KT-465-682

The Trail Breakers

Ray Hardin wasn't well suited to the job, but he was the best man that Glen Wycherly had. It was nearly time for the spring gather of cattle to be hitting the trail, but Wycherly's ranch had followed the same southern trail for years. Every rustler, ne'er-do-well and local Indian knew when and where the herd would pass, and it made for easy pickings.

Wycherly's old map suggests a route through the Pocono Mountains; a route which no one in memory had ridden. Ray and his old partner, Wally Chambers, take to the tangled hills with some reluctance.

Along the way awaits a nest of outlaws, the last of the Jumano Indians, and a young woman who takes a liking to Wally. But the trail into the unknown raises more problems than cattle-rustlers ever could.

By the same author

The Devil's Canyon
The Drifter's Revenge
West of Tombstone
On The Wapiti Range
Rolling Thunder
The Bounty Killers
Six Days to Sundown
Rogue Law
The Land Grabbers
On the Great Plains
Dead Man's Guns
The Legacy
Smuggler's Gulch
The Tanglewood Desperadoes
The Lost Trail
The Killing Time
Travelin' Money
Mystery Herd
Tanglefoot
The Tarnished Badge

The Trail Breakers

Logan Winters

ROBERT HALE · LONDON

First published in Great Britain 2014

ISBN 978-0-7198-1087-9

Robert Hale Limited
Clerkenwell House
Clerkenwell Green
London EC1R 0HT

www.halebooks.com

Typeset by
Derek Doyle & Associates, Shaw Heath
Printed and bound in Great Britain by
CPI Antony Rowe, Chippenham and Eastbourne

ONE

Glen Wycherly owned the Broken W Ranch his father had staked out in the 1840s. He had a herd of 2,000 mixed longhorns and Herefords grazing on the 10,000 acres of dry grassland he claimed down along the Sabine River. That was the problem – in that country he was in danger of overgrazing the voracious steers.

The Broken W had two neat white houses, one for the boss and his family, the other for any relations who might happen by. None ever did in this remote country, but the small house, although it remained empty, was well maintained and kept clean. Wycherly's hope seemed to be that one or more of his four children would marry and choose to live on the Broken W afterward. None of them seemed likely to marry any time soon. Lyle Wycherly, or 'Duke' as he preferred to be called, but seldom was except in jest, was twenty-five years old, at the age when you would think he would start considering marriage. There were a few problems with Duke Wycherly – foremost of which was that women ignored him, laughed at him, or gave him the cold shoulder after one meeting. The younger Wycherly was pretty well set up when it came to physical form and of average dark looks. The trouble with Lyle Wycherly was that he dressed like a fop, rode like a sissy and cursed like a navvy, all of which turned feminine hearts sour.

Glenn Wycherly also had three daughters on the ranch. There was the eldest, Louise, who enjoyed playing lady of the manor. She glided around, usually in black dresses, her hair pinned up, issuing orders to which no one paid any attention before retiring to her room around noon to fan her brow, her day's work done. There weren't many men around who were in the market for that sort of woman, and fewer that she would have found suitable for a lady of her position.

The youngest girl, Josie, appeared to be a pretty little pixie, a child actually, although she was nearly eighteen. In truth she was a pocket-sized hellion. Her copper hair was seldom brushed. She liked to ride, and she rode wildly, carelessly. She loved her dogs of which she had six untrained beasts. She had been known to take on a ranch hand in a wrestling match. In short, she seemed like a long project for any man who might care to try to tame her. Not many suitors returned after their first visit with Josie. A minister from the nearby town of Strasbourg had rushed away nearly in tears after one afternoon tea social meeting.

In between these two daughters was the third, Patricia, who was, to put it bluntly, a plain-looking woman, and she knew it. She was dutiful, sincere, a fine cook. She was also gangly and awkward in her movements, uncertain when she tried to speak. She was fearful of men, tongue-tied when she attempted to talk to one, and given to solitary pursuits only. No one had a bad word to say about Patricia; no one, in fact, ever commented on the girl. She seemed to be marked for perpetual spinsterhood.

Lyle Wycherly, sitting his big white gelding like a knight without armor – or a straw man, take your pick – located Ray Hardin out on Cobblestone Creek where he and three other Broken W hands had been gathering strays, working their horses hard to push the half-wild steers out of the hilly brush country on this hot afternoon.

'I think they get themselves up into that tangle on purpose, just to see how long it will take us to push them out,' Wally Chambers said. Chambers and Ray Hardin had teamed together for a long while. Chambers was small in stature, blue-eyed and blond. When the two were on foot, Ray Hardin, tall and lean with dark curly hair, towered over his saddle partner. On horseback they were pretty much the same size, with Wally being the slightly better roper of the two.

'Our lord and master is here,' Wally said, mopping the perspiration from his throat and face with his blue kerchief. Ray Hardin shifted his eyes to the far bank of the ravine where they had been working and saw the erect figure of Lyle Wycherly sitting his big white horse. Lyle waved a beckoning hand at Ray.

'The Duke commands,' Wally Chambers muttered, tying his kerchief back around his neck. 'I wonder what he wants.'

'I don't know. I wish he would just ride down and tell us like any normal man instead of making me ride up the bluff and back down again.'

'Probably wants to invite you to tea.' Wally smiled and turned his tough little dun horse away to return to the brush-popping. Ray turned toward the path leading up to the rim of the ravine. The dry wind slapped his leather chaps around as he rode his oddly marked brown, black and white paint pony up the narrow trail. Lyle Wycherly sat his horse impatiently.

'Took you a while,' the ranch owner's son said. Ray noticed that the man was improving his speech. He had only managed to insert three four-letter words into that sentence.

'Most things do,' Ray Hardin answered. 'What can I do for you?'

'You?' Lyle's look was appropriately scornful. 'Nothing at all, ever, but my father wants to see you at the house. Immediately.' That speech required five profanities. Ray Hardin decided to quit counting. Lyle Wycherly seemed to have decided that talking that way made him appear more manly, though Hardin knew of not a single man in the bunkhouse who cussed like that. They all knew that it only made you sound like a badly brought-up kid.

'Your father didn't tell you what it was about?' Ray enquired.

'No, and I don't have the time to discuss it.' Lyle attempted a sly smile. 'I'm off to see Virginia Dale over at the Bucket Ranch – you know her, don't you? The one with the. . . .' Hardin had already started his pony away from Lyle Wycherly. The man would never grow up, and in his self-structured wonderland he would never even understand that. Ray pitied old Glen Wycherly, who must have made at least an attempt to bring his son up properly.

Ray looked back along the ravine, but could no longer see Wally Chambers, who had re-entered the tall screen of chaparral brush to try hazing some of those balky steers toward the grass table. The old longhorns took a lot of encouragement to move, which was why it went better when there was a team of men working the job. But Wally was a top hand, and he knew what he was doing on his own.

Half an hour later with the sun riding high, Ray Hardin found himself on the flat where the two white houses sat amid a clustered group of dusty live-oak trees. He chased his shadow into the yard and swung down in front of the big house, lazily looping the reins to the paint pony around and over the hitch rail. A blood-red roan he recognized as belonging to Josie Wycherly was waiting there impatiently.

He considered removing his scarred leather chaps, but decided against it. Glen Wycherly in his forty years on the range had seen many a dusty man in chaps before now. Ray approached the front door with his once-white Stetson in hand and knocked. Unlatched, the door swung open on its own, admitting Hardin to the interior. He had been there often, but was still struck by the height of the ceiling in the drawing room, which rose all the way to the second-story ceiling. The slate-black native-stone fireplace was not quite large enough to roast an ox, but it was impressive, standing six feet wide, four feet high. Wood for a new fire had been set there, awaiting nightfall.

Ray called out, 'Anyone to home? Mister Wycherly!'

'We don't shout in this house,' a stiff feminine voice answered, and Ray, looking to the first landing of the long curved staircase, saw the queen herself, Louise Wycherly, wearing a black dress of some shiny material, her dark hair heaped atop her skull and interwoven with strands of pearls.

'Sorry, Miss Louise. Your father sent for me,' Ray said. The lady of the manor did not reply, she simply lifted her skirt a little, turned her back and proceeded upward to disappear in the upstairs apartments.

Not knowing how to proceed, Ray went near to the unlighted fire and stood, waiting. A hair-raising shriek sounded through the house. This was followed by an animal growl and yap and the thundering of many footsteps on the staircase. The red-haired Josie Wycherly, all five feet of her, wearing range clothes, ran down the stairs followed by her pack of mixed-breed dogs, who followed their mistress in a yapping, howling, snapping jumble of dog flesh, some tripping and tumbling down the stairs, others halting in mid-run to bite at their brothers. Dogs of all coloration and of all breeding snarled, yipped, barked and whined at Josie's heels as she made a mad dash toward the front door, a quirt in her hand. She saw Ray and drew up short, the dogs leaping at her, on each other.

'Father's in there, second door down the hallway,' Josie told Ray. She swatted down a few of the leaping dogs, rapped one mean-looking, bear-shepherd mix that had fixed its eyes on Ray with her quirt and rushed toward the front door where she leaped aboard her roan horse and started it off at a dead run, her yapping, untamed dog pack behind and beside her.

She had left the door flung open and so Ray crossed the Indian-carpeted floor and closed it. Then, with a sigh and a brief reflection on whether having sons or daughters was more of a trial, he walked to the hall off the room which Josie had indicated.

He found Glen Wycherly next to the desk in his study, hovering over an unrolled topographical map. The old man glanced up.

'Hello, Ray,' he said in greeting. 'I was hoping Lyle could find you out there. Come here; I want you to have a look at something.'

Glen Wycherly was looking his age this day. Tall, but bent over, his white hair in disarray, his blue eyes excited but dim. Long creases were carved into his tanned cheeks by sun, weather and time. His stubby finger tapped the map he had been studying.

'Do you know what this is, Ray?'

Stepping nearer, Ray studied the map. 'Looks like the Pocono country. Those hills are in the Holden Range.'

'You're right, of course. Does anything strike you wrong about this map?' Glen Wycherly asked.

'I don't know if I'd call it wrong,' Ray Hardin answered, 'but it doesn't go very far, does it?' His finger traced the vast empty center of the map. 'Unknown land,' the cartographer had written in neat pen strokes.

'That's exactly it,' Glen said. He walked across the room, his steps a shuffle, went to the liquor cabinet and removed a bottle of Tennessee whiskey. 'The map's fine as far as it goes, but it just doesn't go far enough.'

'I imagine that's because for years that was a Mescalero Apache stronghold,' Ray ventured. 'Until General Crook got serious about driving them to Mexico. Not many men would have ventured deep onto the Poconos with the exception of a few bad men on the run.'

'Yes,' Glen Wycherly said. Returning, he handed a cut-crystal glass with two fingers of whiskey in it to Ray. Wycherly looked satisfied as he settled behind his broad walnut desk. Ray still didn't get it. Why had Wycherly summoned him to his office?

The ranch owner sipped his drink, nodded with satisfaction at the taste, and placed both hands flat on his desk. He looked up at Ray. 'They tell me that you once worked as a surveyor, Hardin.'

Ray had to laugh. 'Not exactly, sir. I was a stick man with the railroad for about six months.'

'A stick man?'

'His job is to stand out in the hot sun holding a stick while the surveyor behind his transit moves him left, right, forward and back while he gets his line right. It wasn't much of a job as far as I was concerned.'

'But you picked up some basic knowledge of surveying – in six months on the job?'

'A fair amount. I was thinking of going to work as a surveyor. The pay was good with the railroads, but I couldn't take the apprenticeship – I prefer working with a horse between my legs.'

'Can you draw a relief map?' Wycherly wanted to know.

'After a fashion, yes,' Ray answered, still not knowing where the conversation was going.

'Fine, fine,' Wycherly said, finishing his whiskey. He went to the sideboard to pour himself another drink and, with his back to Ray Hardin, went on, 'I've got a contract to deliver five hundred steers to Fort Davis within three months. To feed the soldiers and bargain with the Indians.'

This was nothing new. Broken W had been an army supplier for years, Only the year before Ray Hardin had ridden through with a trail herd to Fort Davis, though nothing like five hundred steers were along. He remembered the drive well: dry, arduous, being confronted by Indians and gangs of white rustlers as well.

Wycherly had resumed his seat at the desk. 'Hardin, if a man could cut five hundred miles off that trip, remove the necessity of skirting the foot of the Holden Range, would you not say it was worth it?'

'Of course.'

Wycherly rose heavily to his feet and went again to the map table. 'Straight through the Poconos,' the ranch boss said, drawing a line with his finger. 'It would save an immense amount of time, and we could avoid the various predators who haunt that southern trail and know when we have a drive mounted.'

'But. . .' Ray didn't know what to say. 'No one has ever ridden through there, let alone try to drive a herd of cattle through. Is there enough water? Any graze?

Are the Indians truly cleared out of the hills? Is that country still infested with thieves and thugs running from the law? Are there passes capable of allowing such a large herd to get through? Is there really any possible trail at all?'

Wycherly was once again seated in his chair. He nodded, sipped at his whiskey and told Ray Hardin, 'Exactly – you have just defined the job I want you to do for me. Find out, Hardin. Get up into that country and use your surveyor's eye to find a trail through – if there is one.'

'But—' Ray began to object.

'I know, "but". I have considered all of them. There is no answer to any of those questions unless someone takes a look. If it can't be done' – Wycherly shrugged – 'then it can't be. But, damn it, Hardin, I want to know. I've been sweating bullets over this contract. A route through the Poconos, if it can be found, might be enough to save the Broken W.'

Ray would never have guessed that the ranch was in any sort of financial trouble, but then again, he knew nothing about the operations of the ranch as a business. Here, too, he was only a stick man, not privy to the decision-making process or the reasoning behind it.

He worked for the brand. Ray said, 'I'll try it, Mr Wycherly. I can't guarantee—'

'Of course you can't,' Glen Wycherly said. Nevertheless he was smiling, appeared relieved. 'You can choose a pack horse from the string and draw whatever supplies you need from our larder. I expect you'll be wanting some help.'

'Since my head is not mounted on a swivel, I'd appreciate having someone along to watch my back. I'd like to take Wally Chambers with me, if you can spare him.'

'Chambers? Has he had some experience surveying?'

'No, sir. But he is reliable, and he is my friend. I don't care for the idea of riding into wild country with someone who is not both.'

'All right,' Wycherly agreed. He stood to shake hands with Ray as a side door to the room opened a bare few inches. 'It's agreed. Patricia!' he called, and the door opened wider to allow Wycherly's third daughter to enter the office.

Wycherly said, 'Patricia will see that you're supplied with paper, drawing pencils, a straight edge and compass – poor tools for what I'm asking you to do, but they're all we have at hand.'

Patricia Wycherly was tall, not so tall as Ray Hardin, of course, but tall for a woman. Her face was pale, her eyes were averted. He noticed that her chin was a little too sharp for classic beauty. Her mouth was drawn tight in what could have been interpreted as a disapproving expression, but Ray, who had met the woman a few times before, knew that it was just her constant fear of human interaction which caused her to appear that way. She was a mouse, looking for a hole in which to escape from the predators of this earth.

Glen Wycherly seemed not to notice, or maybe it was simply familiarity with Patricia's ways. He just said, 'Patricia, Mr Hardin is in need of a few supplies. They should all be found in the library – pencils, paper, compass and straight edge. Do you have all that?'

'It's a simple instruction,' Patricia said, speaking to the floor. Her dark eyes flickered once to Ray Hardin. 'If you will follow me.' Her voice, her expression, her movements were those of a schoolteacher, perhaps a frustrated one who was unhappily resigned to her life. A thought lifted Glen Wycherly's head before they could turn away toward the library.

'Tell Santiago to leave the pantry unlocked, Patricia. These men will need some provisions. Let them have their pick.' The woman nodded, inclined her head and led Ray out into the narrow hall beyond. He said nothing to her. She was not the sort of woman you struck up a conversation with about trivial matters.

As they neared the library, the darkly regal form of Louise Wycherly appeared in the doorway. She cast a disparaging glance at Ray – or at her sister, perhaps both – and swept away, her black skirts rustling. It was incredible that such a beautiful woman should choose to distance herself from the world. Maybe it was her beauty that prompted her aloofness.

'Everything you need should be found in that wall cabinet,' Patricia said. Her voice faltered. She was so painfully shy that Ray found himself pitying her. She stood aside as Ray rummaged through the supplies in the cabinet, apparently unsure of whether she was supposed to stay and supervise or rush away.

'This should do it,' Ray said, closing the cupboard. 'It's not much to work with, is it?'

He hadn't expected an answer, got none. Once into the hallway again, the heavy door to the library closed, Patricia turned away sharply and walked in the direction her older sister had taken, leaving Ray Hardin alone in the disturbing atmosphere of the Wycherly house. He started toward the front door. Knowing no other route to take, he again entered Glen Wycherly's office, finding the old man with a fresh glass of whiskey at his elbow, his furrowed face in his hands.

Glancing up he said, 'Got what you need, Hardin? Good. I have hopes that you can find a Pocono pass, but no real expectations. That is, do this for me if you can; if it can't be done, there will be no blame attached to you. Just another of an old man's . . . just one more notion that didn't pan out.'

There was nothing to be said to that. Ray just nodded and went out of the house. Glen Wycherly looked older than he had that morning. Time was running hard after him. Or, Ray wondered as he swung aboard his paint pony, was it only the ranch that worried him? Could his own children be driving him to an early grave? They certainly were a rare collection.

After stowing the mapping supplies in the bunkhouse, Ray set out for the gather again to pull Wally Chambers off the job. Wally would not like it – he was a man who wanted to finish a task once he was given one. An admirable trait, but Ray Hardin wanted both Wally and his horse fresh for their morning start into the Pocono Mountains. Or *hills.* It depended on where you were from. To a man from the high-up Colorado mountain country where peaks sprouted to a grand height of 14,000 feet and more, the Poconos would seem like nothing more than pimples on the land. To a low-ranger from Kansas, the Poconos would appear tall, tangled, savage and daunting.

Ray walked his horse along the rim of the ravine to where he had last seen Wally Chambers at work and eventually found him. He let out a loud, shrill whistle and watched Wally's head turn his way. He waved in a way which was not commanding, but showed some urgency. After a minute he saw Wally turn his dun horse's head and start toward him.

Glancing around, Ray saw a small herd of steers and an equally small collection of year-old calves grazing on the dry grass. These were kept separate since the yearlings would not be joining them on a trail drive. The calves, still gangly and clumsy, had also been separated from the cows, some of which would be hitting the trail with the herd. The calves were milling, bawling, frisking according to their temperaments, all suffering growing pains.

Ray could identify two of the three men circling the herd, coiled lariats in their hands. The easy-going Travis Knight and the more excitable Lenny Polk. They had the gravy job this afternoon – simply keeping the gathered cattle together, keeping them calm.

That was when a whirlwind arose to the north. There was something akin to an Indian war-whoop, a horse being driven wildly toward them, a pack of baying hounds behind the rider. Josie Wycherly was headed home. Using her quirt steadily on her winded red roan she stormed toward the herd, through it and past it. Her Stetson was hanging down her back from its drawstring, and her red hair streamed wildly in the wind. A few of the dogs had enough energy left to snap their jaws at the calves in passing. The rest lagged, their tongues hanging out in total exhaustion.

Lenny Polk waved his arms excitedly and shouted something unheard and pointless to the skies. The older Travis Knight placidly began pushing the young beeves into a tight bunch again. It was all a part of the job to Knight, if not to Lenny Polk, who had not been long on the Broken W. If any cowboy had tried such a stunt, Lenny would have ridden after him, formed a loop in his lariat and roped the man from his horse's back and hog-tied him before beginning to instruct him on proper ranch behavior.

No one was going to rope and tie Josie Wycherly, and she knew it. Perhaps no one could.

'I saw a part of that,' Wally Chambers said, approaching over the lip of the ravine. 'What happened?' He had removed his hat and was mopping the perspiration from his forehead. The day remained hot.

'Just Josie riding home.'

'Oh, that's what I figured – all I could see was a cloud of dust from where I was.' Chambers replaced his hat, wagged his head. 'How would you like to be the man who tried to train that one?'

'I prefer simpler tasks – that's why I called you up, Wally. We're going trail-breaking.'

'We are?' Wally Chambers eyed Ray dubiously. 'Where?'

'Straight through the Poconos,' Ray Hardin told him, lifting his chin toward the not-so-distant mass of white mountains.

'We are, are we?' Wally said, his face dour. 'You know

there's likely no graze to be had there, no known water source?'

'I know,' Ray said, attempting a grin.

'And you do know that there's supposed to be an outlaw stronghold hidden away in those hills?'

'Yes.'

'And no one is sure that the Apaches have cleared out entirely?'

'I do. That's what we're supposed to find out,' Ray Hardin told his smaller, blond companion.

Wally scratched his neck thoughtfully, looked toward the mountains and then said, 'Oh, hell, if that's what we're going to do, let's have at it, Ray.'

TWO

The larder had been left open, and that evening Ray Hardin and Wally Chambers took no little time going through the food stores. They had no idea how long their journey might take, and going hungry was the last thing they needed to worry about.

Wally began loading five-pound sacks of dried pinto beans into the burlap bag at his feet. Ray pulled him up short.

'Beans take a time to boil. We won't be wanting to start many cook fires up in that country, Wally, or be lingering long over meals.'

Slightly crestfallen, the young cowhand said regretfully, 'They have everything I need for doctoring those beans up properly.' Which meant there was a bin of onions and string of red peppers hanging from the ceiling. Wally's concept of fixing beans was creative and expansive to say the least. It was a toss-up as to whether the beans he used weighed more than the spices added. Ray had heard Wally say once: 'I don't mind the way these Mexicans fix their food, but it seems that they are shy when it comes to spicing it up.'

Ray watched as Wally reluctantly let the onions tumble back into the bin. 'Let's just keep it simple, Wally. Basic food and as much as we can carry. You might snag one of those hanging hams,' he suggested.

He was interrupted in the next moment by an intrusive voice: 'Just what in hell are you two doing in here? You know the pantry is off-limits to ranch hands!'

Enough expletives were sprinkled into the challenge to announce the owner of the voice as Lyle Wycherly.

'Your father told us to get what we needed,' Ray Hardin said blandly. He didn't like a single thing about Duke Wycherly, but tried not to let it show and affect his relationship with the ranch.

'Get what you need for what?' Lyle demanded. 'A winter in the Yukon?' He nodded toward the over-full burlap bags at Ray and Wally's feet.

'We're taking a trip into the Poconos – it might be quite a long trek,' Ray responded evenly.

Lyle wasn't through fuming yet. The young man stood with his back arched, face flushed, his freshly sprouted mustache quivering on his upper lip. His hands were actually bunched into fists, not menacingly, but as if with childish frustration.

'The Poconos! Why?'

'I think your father has some idea about trying to drive a herd straight through to Fort Davis using that route – if there is one.'

'But we've never gone that way,' an angry and exasperated Lyle Wycherly complained. 'We've always taken the southern route.'

'And been robbed blind along the way,' Wally Chambers chipped in.

'This is unacceptable,' Lyle said, keeping his voice just below a shout.

Ray Hardin shrugged. 'Talk to your father, then. If he wants to call the job off, it's no skin off our chins.'

'I'll do just that!' Lyle Wycherly spun on his heel and stalked out of the pantry, through the kitchen and on into the interior of the house.

'What now?' Wally asked.

'Continue doing what we were told to do – plenty of corn meal and a side of bacon, and any handy tinned goods. . . .' Ray paused. Wally was doing something with his fingers.

At Ray's questioning expression, Wally said, 'How many did you count?'

'How many?' Ray got it then. 'I've given up counting with that man.'

'Twenty-one cusswords I counted,' Wally said. 'Maybe he's trying to go for a new record.'

And even for Lyle Wycherly that was a lot of excited expletives over nothing at all. It gave Ray pause to consider. Wally had shouldered a heavy burlap sack. Now he said quite thoughtfully, 'I think I'll shoot the bastard one day.'

'All right,' Ray answered, not entirely certain if Wally was kidding or not. For himself, if the day came when Lyle Wycherly became boss of the Broken W, Ray was set to ride off the ranch and not look back.

The stolid off-white mule with her reddish-brown mane and tail which Ray had selected from the ranch's pack animals stood for their loading of travel provisions without complaint. Someone had named her Bess, and she was typical of her breed: placid, sturdy, willing to help but utterly unmovable if she sensed the threat of danger ahead. Not bad qualities. Ray had seen a horse or two determine in its own mind to stamp and kill a rattlesnake encountered on the trail. A mule would simply halt in its tracks and refuse to move until the danger was past. Having a skittish animal along was no drawback in the country they were going to where the animal might sense danger of which its human masters were unaware.

And there were said to be many unknown dangers in the Poconos. Matters that Glen Wycherly needed to have determined before sending a valuable herd of cattle into the white hills. Wycherly knew that his scouts might not return from that country where outlaws were reported to have their secret roost and where Apaches were rumored to still occupy at least a part of the country.

Whatever happened to Wally and Ray Hardin, it was going to be no picnic up in those savage hills.

The canvas army bags they strapped onto Bess's back contained nearly 500 rounds of .44-.40 ammunition – enough to start a small graveyard – and four spare Colt revolvers. Ray Hardin was taking nothing for granted. He armed them as if they were going to war. Perhaps they were. Crook's army might have driven the Apaches away, but certainly no lawmen had ever risked riding into the remote Poconos to try to clean out the robbers' roosts. These represented a serious threat. Outlaws needed beef, too, and they knew full well how to sell off rustled steers. Ray could only hope that the rumors of the outlaws' presence were only that. Things had been bad enough for trail drives along the southern route; to be trapped in narrow canyons in the far mountains would be too much to expect a bunch of cowboys to fight their way out of.

'Want to say goodbye to anybody?' Ray Hardin asked, checking the cinches on his own saddle once more.

Wally laughed. 'No, but I wish I'd had the time to write out a will – what's going to happen to my seven silver dollars after I'm gone?'

There was already color in the western sky when they had finished loading their camp goods on Bess. It was really too late to be starting out, but Ray was anxious to get away from the ranch for some reason he could not define. The trail was well marked for a few miles, and Ray knew from studying the incomplete map Glen Wycherly had given him where he intended to go. An early start, an early camp, a good night's sleep with a fresh morning before them sounded good to Ray.

There would be little need for scouting work in the first few days. The cartographer – whoever he had been – had mapped the land precisely. What had happened to this old map-maker, Ray Hardin wondered, and why hadn't he continued farther into the Poconos? There could be a dozen reasons, none of which mattered at the present.

Wally Chambers had tightened down the last strap on Bess's burden and checked the cinches of his saddled dun horse. Ray had returned from the well with the two five-gallon casks he had been filling. They carried two half-gallon canteens each as well; the extra water was for the animals should they go luckless in finding water in the hills. That was one commodity they could not run short on. Ray lowered the casks which he had been carrying with canvas straps across his shoulders and straightened up, stretching his back.

The hesitant dark shadow appeared on the back porch of the big house and took three determined strides toward Ray. Patricia Wycherly did not look up as she handed a small muslin sack to Ray.

'I thought you might forget these,' she said in a murmur. 'I mean, men. . . .' That was all the painful shyness of Patricia Wycherly would allow her to say. She scurried away, moving stiffly, anxiously. Wally Chambers emerged from behind the dun. There was a grin on his face.

'A gift from the lady?' he asked.

'Shut up, Wally.'

'Have you gone and charmed her with your manliness?'

'Didn't you hear me?' Ray said.

'Oh, I heard you,' Wally said, removing his hat to wipe back his yellow hair. 'Has it gotten to where you can't take a joke? What's in the sack?'

'I'm just looking, if you'll be quiet,' Ray said, feeling irritable for some reason. Loosening the drawstring on the small sack, he examined its contents. 'Heh?' he exclaimed, holding one item up.

'What's that?' Wally asked.

'One of those boar's bristle toothbrushes.'

'I always use a green twig myself,' Wally said.

'Well, so do I, but I suppose it might be useful.'

'What else is in there, Ray?'

Hardin was examining a small tin with a decorated lid. He squinted at it, sniffed the can and replied, 'Some sort of tooth powder, it says. Smells kind of like mint.' He waved the tooth powder under Wally's nose. Wally Chambers still appeared amused.

'What else?' Wally prodded.

'Just this,' Ray said, pulling a squarish block of yellow lye soap from the bag before replacing the items and pulling the drawstring tight.

'Oh, my friend, you are in trouble,' Wally said.

'What are you talking about? It's just some things that, as she said, a man wouldn't ordinarily think of but a woman does.'

'First step a woman takes in corralling a man,' Wally said, with a sad, insincere shake of his head. 'First thing they want to do is clean a man up – maybe buy him a new shirt or a razor. Yes, Ray, you have somehow charmed the woman.'

'I explained that already – she just wanted us to have a few extra trail supplies we might not have thought of.' Ray was growing testy and he knew it. Wally swung aboard his dun horse, looked down and winked.

'Then, Ray, where is *my* new, boar's bristle toothbrush?'

'I suppose we're meant to share it,' Ray grumbled. He took the reins to his paint pony, handed the leads to the mule to Wally, and swung into leather himself.

'Because,' Wally said as they kneed their horses

forward at a walk, 'you know when a woman has her sights set on you—'

'Wally?'

'What?'

'How many times do I have to tell you to shut up?'

With sunset coloring the skies beyond, they rode slowly through the stand of live-oak trees clustered around the Wycherly house. There were two riders sitting their ponies in the darkness of the grove, waiting for them. One of them called out, 'Hold up, Hardin!'

They knew the voice. It was Brian Akers, a man they had both worked with often. His bulky partner, now that they drew nearer, could be identified as well. Sully Parks, an overweight, sullen troublemaker who thought he intimidated men with his bulk alone.

'What do you want, Brian?' Ray Hardin asked cautiously, seeing that both of the men they faced now had their rifles unsheathed and positioned across their saddlebows.

'Well, Hardin, we got the word that you're not to go anywhere off the ranch,' Akers said.

'Not alive,' the thick-shouldered Sully Parks said venomously.

'Who says so?' Wally Chambers challenged.

'Duke Wycherly, that's who!' Parks spat back. 'You might have heard of him – he's boss of the Broken W.'

'Since when?' Hardin asked. 'Listen, boys, we have our orders from Glen Wycherly, we're acting under *his* instructions.'

Brian Akers's eyebrows lowered and doubt crept into his expression. 'Is that straight, Ray?'

'It's straight – what did you think we were doing?'

'Stealing away with a Broken W animal and a load of supplies from the larder.'

'Was I to rustle stock,' Wally Chambers said, sitting his horse easily, 'it wouldn't be an old mule that I took.' Wally's hand, Ray noticed if the two men facing them had not, had dropped down much closer to his holstered Colt.

'We got our orders,' Sully Parks complained to Akers. 'If we don't take 'em back, Duke will be—'

'You can try to stop us,' Wally Chambers said in a cool voice – the one he used when he was not kidding. 'Of course if you do, I'll shoot you out of the saddle, Sully.' Wally's hand was now resting on the butt of his pistol and the other men had noticed it.

'Hell, Wally,' Sully said, in a taut, fearful voice, 'you and I rode a lot of trails together. We've been good saddle partners.'

'We used to be,' Wally Chambers replied. 'Now I'm just a wild-eyed thief, a desperate man.'

Brian Akers knew that Wally meant it. He tried to calm the situation. 'Leave it, Sully. We didn't come out here to get in no gunfight. We'll go back and tell Duke that we delivered his message to these two.'

'Then what?' Sully asked fearfully.

'Then I guess we'll get cussed out, but we won't have any new holes in our bodies.'

Ray Hardin said, 'I think that's probably the better idea, Akers.'

Akers nodded his head, gestured to Sully Parks and started his horse back through the oak grove toward the

Wycherly house.

There was a silver half-moon floating high above the Poconos when the two entered the rough country. There was still a bare hint of color along the western horizon, and the coming moon provided some light as they made their way steadily into the white hills. The trail was easy for the three animals, but Ray Hardin continually gauged it for the width a herd of five hundred steers would need. Even well strung out, this way would be some trouble for a bunch that size. The trail, he knew, widened out as they came to the low crest and started downward again. He had been pretty much able to memorize the map he had been shown in Wycherly's office.

It was the unknown land ahead that presented a challenge.

All of the color had faded from the sky. The stars not blurred by the coming moon were winking brightly when, two hours on, Ray and Wally Chambers came to the shelf of land where Ray had planned to spend their first night on the trail. The map was accurate in every respect and they had no trouble riding up to and along the bench where they would have a clear view of the trail below, and in the morning of the tangled, barren land ahead.

'This is it?' Wally asked, looking around at the moon-bright shelf jutting from the white hills. There was a screen of mesquite trees on two sides, the white bluff on the third. Some stunted nopal cactus grew near the face of the rising cliff.

'This is it – I didn't plan on putting many miles

behind us on this first night,' Ray Hardin answered.

'It looks fine to me,' Wally said, swinging down. 'Flat ground, good view all around us. Not much fodder for the animals, but they were just fed when we left, and if they have a taste for them, they can scrounge for mesquite beans.'

Ray agreed silently. His main concern now was watching to find out if they were being followed – and trying to figure out why, if so. Brian Akers and Sully had been far too interested in keeping them out of the Poconos. Lyle Wycherly had been equally troublesome earlier. What business was it of theirs where Ray and Wally rode?

Unburdening the mule, they made a rough camp on the shelf of dry earth. There was a pleasant southerly breeze to keep the insects down, though as far as they were now from any standing water, there would have been few flying critters to annoy them anyway.

Wally, chow-dog that he was, did not feel like building a cook-fire on this night. Using his belt knife, he pried open a tin of stewed tomatoes from their plentiful supplies and ate them with some of the salt biscuits they had taken from the cook's stock and a few strips of peppery jerky, followed with deep drinks of his canteen water. Pronouncing himself satisfied, Wally stretched out on his back beneath his blankets, hands behind his head, and looked skyward.

'This is nothing but a picnic, so far,' Wally said.

'It's the "so far" that worries me. We have no idea where we're going, who else might be there, and who might be dogging our trail.'

'You always were a worrier, Ray. We take it one day at a time – there's nothing else to do.' Wally lifted his head a little. 'Do you really think there's somebody following us?'

'It's more that I think that someone will be.'

'Like Sully and Brian?'

'Them or someone else. Sully and Brian' – Ray shook his head – 'they were almost willing to go to gunplay to keep us from starting out.'

Ray Hardin sat down on his own bed and tugged his boots off as Wally watched. He waited until Ray was rolled up in his blankets and settled before he asked, 'Why, Ray? To keep us from finding a trail to the fort? Who wouldn't want to make the trail drive a shorter proposition?'

'Someone who profited more from the long, south-trail route.'

'You mean someone who might be in league with those hold-up gangs down that way?'

'I don't know who I mean,' Ray said with a touch of irritation. He was tired and his back ached from a day in the saddle. Was he already growing too old for this sort of work? 'But, we know that Lyle Wycherly sent those two to warn us off.'

'Duke!' Wally laughed without humor. 'Why in hell would he want to undermine the Broken W? He'll be the owner of the ranch before too many years.'

'Maybe,' Ray responded.

'Maybe? Of course he will after Glen Wycherly is gone.'

'There are three other children,' Ray pointed out.

Wally laughed again. 'Oh, yeah, I'm sure Glen would leave the ranch he spent years building up to a crazy little hellion like Josie Wycherly.'

'Then not Josie. What about Louise?'

'She doesn't know what work is; doesn't know how the ranch functions. She likely couldn't find any men willing to work for her.' Wally was thoughtfully silent for a moment. 'That leaves Patricia, doesn't it? She's a loyal daughter, steady, devoted to her duties. . . .' There was a pause. 'That reminds me, Ray, did you remember to brush your teeth?'

'I'll kill you someday, Wally,' Ray Hardin grunted.

'Partner, there's a line of men a mile long who've promised to do that. I guess I'm just not lovable.'

'I guess not,' Ray agreed.

'But, even thinking the way we were, Ray, that still doesn't answer the question of why Duke or any of the girls would wish to bring the Broken W down.'

'Maybe to get what they can while the getting is good. No waiting for Glen to pass away. If that nest of robbers and cattle thieves along the southern route was tipped off in advance about our trail drives, there could be a split agreed to. Half of the stolen cattle for the information. In this case that would net the informant two hundred or more cattle that could be easily driven to Mexico for sale. And Lyle – let's say it was Lyle – would not be risking anything.'

'That would be a lot of pocket money,' Wally said around a yawn. 'Something like stealing from Glen Wycherly's wallet.'

'Could have been going on for years, for all we know.

Maybe Glen has seen his books lately and realized they have a problem on the Broken W.'

'I guess it could be. You still awake, Ray? This brings to mind the Blue Moon-KL trouble up in Colorado. You ever hear about that?'

'Tell me,' Ray said, too sleepy now to care.

'Jack "Blue Moon" Priest was running a pretty powerful gang outside of Pueblo, Colorado. The gang was made up of . . . oh, you don't care about all their names just now, but there are a lot of stories attached to those men. Jack Priest, he had a deal with a local rancher's son. The King Lawrence ranch I'm talking about.

'It wasn't really their game, but Jack Priest's crowd turned to rustling in a big way. King Lawrence, he was losing ten, twenty, thirty steers a night off his range. KL couldn't find any more men to hire on – no one wanted to ride for that brand. Wranglers, night-herd riders were picked off one by one as they tried to go about their business. Must have been ten, twelve men murdered on the range, and the cattle kept being driven off.

'Finally old King Lawrence found himself teetering on the edge of bankruptcy. Had no assets remaining, and the bank eventually foreclosed on KL. He died a broken man.

'Three months later the ranch went up for sale and King's son came forward to rescue the property. By the next year the KL was thriving again. Cattle kept being driven back onto the range. Some of them seemed mighty familiar with the land, if you understand me.'

'A lot of the stolen cattle were driven back onto the

range,' Ray said, himself stifling a yawn now.

'Exactly. Wasn't that a filthy deed to pull on your own father? But some people have no conscience at all.'

'Are we still talking about Lyle Wycherly?' Ray asked.

'I don't know; are we? It depends on who we catch following us up into these mountains. Things may be clearer by the light of day.' Again there was a pause while Ray drifted nearer to sleep. Wally had to have the last word:

'Are you sure you brushed your teeth, Ray?'

THREE

The morning sun was low and hot, even at this altitude. Wally Chambers was first up and had busied himself starting a small, mesquite-wood camp-fire. Ray Hardin found himself thanking his stars that his trail-mate was amenable to cooking. Ham had been sliced and fried and now there were corn pone cakes on the griddle.

'Ten minutes or so,' Wally announced from his crouched position over the fire. Ray Hardin stretched his arms, greeting the new day, his eyes searching the land before them.

'That's about enough time to water the horses and the mule – unless you've already done that too.'

'No,' Wally said, smiling. 'A man can only do so much.'

Ray poured water from one of the heavy casks they had been carrying into a galvanized bucket to offer to the horses individually. Fortunately each of the animals was patient enough to wait its turn. After a few more days on the trail, would that patience hold? With the job finished, Ray sauntered back to the camp-fire where

Wally was already finishing his meager but sustaining breakfast of ham and pone cakes.

'Forgive my manners,' Wally said, looking up at Ray.

'You cooked it, you deserve to eat first,' Ray said, reaching for his own tin plate and fork. Wally had something on his mind. He rose, glanced toward the stock and then across the white land ahead.

'They passed by us in the night, Ray. Did you hear anything?'

'Nothing,' Ray said, stopping with his fork halfway to his mouth. 'What do you mean? Who passed us? And how do you know?'

'I woke up sometime after midnight, by the stars. I needed some relief. I could smell dust heavy in the air. I looked but couldn't see no horses in the darkness, but someone passed by on the road, riding east.'

'You sound sure.'

'I'm sure – I've smelled dust before,' Wally answered with a little smile. 'And there wasn't any wind blowing to stir it up.'

'I wonder who. . . ?' Ray said, letting the sentence drop away.

'Well, let's see,' Wally Chambers said with mock consideration as he rolled up his blankets. 'They came up from the west – now what's down there beside the Broken W Ranch?'

'Nothing at all,' Ray said, helping Wally with his game.

'Gosh – do you think it could have been somebody from the Broken W who already warned us not to come up here?'

'Knock it off, Wally, I get you,' Ray Hardin said. 'I just don't know why anyone would want to stop us badly enough to trail after us in the dark.'

'Is that what worries you, Ray?' Wally asked, tying up his bedroll and rising. 'What worries me more is how far they're willing to go to keep us from continuing on.'

By the time they broke camp it was somewhere near eight o'clock. They eased the horses down the trail from the bench and began automatically scanning the loose white soil on the road for signs of passage. The tracks of the night travelers weren't that difficult to spot. Even in the powdery earth, the evidence of three passing horses was evident. One animal had marked its route definitely.

'Had to be Lyle Wycherly, Sully and Brian Akers, don't you think?' Wally asked. That was the assumption both men had reached.

'Seems so – can you read sign well enough to make out the imprints of the horses' shoes?' Ray asked.

'In this soil?' Wally laughed. 'I'm no army scout or Indian tracker. I doubt either could tell you anything from these indefinite tracks – even if they had made a study of the shoes of the three horses those men rode – and I have never bothered myself with that.'

'No, I know,' Ray said. 'There's nothing for it but to ride on and keep our eyes and ears open, is there?'

'Not that I can think of to suggest,' Wally replied.

The first morning on the trail passed easily. Ray continued to find that the map he carried folded in his saddle-bags and consulted when they paused along the trail was very accurate. The first half of the trip was relative child's play. He could see why Glen Wycherly had become interested in a possible route through the Poconos after studying the map. The trails were broad, the low areas covered with a meager growth of grass.

It was what lay beyond the map's scope in the area labeled as 'unknown land' that serious problems might lie.

Ahead now, as they rode higher on the shoulders of the white hills rising above them, lay a crucial point. On the map there was a spot marked as Indian Springs, but Ray knew well that these springs in arid country came and went dry frequently. Was there still a source of water there – enough for a herd the size Glen Wycherly was planning on driving through?

There was no telling. The two men rode on, among the jumble of white formations thrust up eons ago by earth tremors. The sun was high and hot, the air motionless. Both men had shed their leather chaps. They expected to do no riding through heavy chaparral.

'Where's this place supposed to be?' Wally Chambers asked just before midday.

'Not far – somewhere beyond that flat hill ahead.'

'Ray? I hate to ask, but aren't you supposed to be drawing a map or something?'

'No need to yet. The one we have is smack on.'

'You riding with your eyes open anyway?' Wally asked. Ray knew what he meant. He had not seen any sign of other riders in the hills, though from time to time they came across blurred tracks. All they could tell from these hoofprints was that the horses were shod, meaning that the odds were low that they belonged to any passing Indians. Which was all for the good. The last thing they needed out here was to meet up with some hold-out Mescalero Apaches.

It was almost with awe that they crested the low hump on the trail and looked down upon the valley. The spring itself would be higher up in the barren hills, but it had fathered a wide-running creek which made its serpentine way across the flats. There was grass, many acres of it sprouting there, bright green and appealing.

'I thought we were talking about a sporadic little mountain spring,' Wally Chambers said, tilting back his hat.

'So did I,' Ray Hardin admitted. 'Think that's enough graze for five hundred steers, Wally?'

'Yes, in passing,' the blond cowboy answered. 'Probably wouldn't be enough to set up ranching here, the way those cattle can mow grass. But sure, for a stopover along the way, it would suit.'

'I think so, too.' Although the map had not depicted this grassy valley as such, and why would it? His – the cartographer's – interest was in landforms, not vegetation – it only stood to reason. The Apaches would have needed enough water for their tribe's requirements and grass for their horses as well. This would have been the place where they made camp. Ray saw no signs left from the Apache occupation, but then it had been a while since they flourished here, and the Mescaleros were basically nomadic, leaving little permanent behind them when they left.

'We going down?' Wally asked. 'Or sitting here enjoying the view?'

'We're going down. It's along our way.'

'Our way where?' Wally asked, as they started their horses down the slope. 'I hate to mention it, but we don't even know if there is a pass out of these hills to the east.'

'If there isn't, the troops at Fort Davis will just have to wait a while longer for their beef.'

When they reached the flat land and walked their horses slowly across the grass, Ray watched the inviting silver and blue sparkle of the creek and said, 'A bath wouldn't be unwelcome, seeing as we have the chance.'

'No, it wouldn't. Just make sure you're downstream from the animals if you plan on using that bar of lye soap, Ray. Might poison them.'

'I'll watch it,' Ray told his partner. 'And I'll be sure to save some soap for you.'

'Me?' Wally said. 'Oh, I wouldn't want to use any of your personal soap which Miss Patricia gave to you. It's you she wants to smell better, Ray!'

'Wally. . . .' Ray warned.

'I know – shut up.' Wally chuckled a little. 'Do you want me to ride up and have a look at the spring, make sure it isn't in danger of clogging up from land fall and such?'

'You'd better, I suppose,' Ray said, swinging down from the paint's back. 'I'd hate to ride back and report that there was a good quantity of water here and then find it had dried up before Wycherly could reach it.'

Such springs in open country could be clogged by the uncertain movements of the land around them, fallen rocks or an aggregate of brush. Even if it could be cleaned out later, it would delay the herd and cause a lot of grumbling among the men dispatched to clear the spring, who considered any work that could not be done from horseback to be beneath them.

Wally rode his dun horse out toward the headwaters of the river as Ray slipped the bit from his paint, loosed the lead line from Bess's muzzle and led them to water. Then, while the animals grazed contentedly on the young grass, Ray removed the bar of yellow lye soap from his saddle-bags, stripped off his clothes and walked toward the river.

To hell with Wally and his caustic remarks, a man deserved to be as clean as he could keep himself. It had nothing to do with Patricia Wycherly. He thought briefly of the plain woman as he stood in the water bathing. The shy Patricia was intelligent, loyal, thoughtful and practical. Why weren't men attracted to those qualities in a woman? He wasn't smart enough to answer his own question. It was only flash, flair and beauty that attracted them, like dance-hall girls in their silks and finery – yet how often did any of them ever last as a life's companion? Never. They were more devoted to their own appearance than to any man.

If only Patricia had some of her sister Louise's beauty, some of the reckless flair and humor of Josie Wycherly . . . that train of thought could lead nowhere. Ray waded from the river and tugged his clothes on.

He refitted his paint pony and settled Bess's load once again. There was still a lot of daylight remaining. He took the map from his saddle-bags and examined again, briefly. They had now reached the limit of the cartographer's survey. The land beyond was now *terra incognita*, as primitive and alien as ever.

It was not the broad white land that was daunting, it was the men they might find among the pale hills. It was a mystery as to why Lyle Wycherly and his sidekicks – Sully and Brian Akers? – had ridden past them and continued on if they had been trailing Wally and Ray. Perhaps Lyle had some other destination in mind, which would mean he knew the Poconos much better than he had admitted.

Rumors of an outlaw town, a robber's roost, being located up here swirled around in Ray's mind without settling anywhere. He shook his head to try to clear it; probably imagination was running wild. At any rate he had a job to do and daydreaming was not going to get it done. He walked back to a flat, semi-circular patch of grassland he had spotted and settled in to await Wally's return from the spring.

Growing impatient, hungry, Ray broke down and fixed himself a small noon meal of ham, biscuits and tinned yams from their supplies. Leaving half for Wally, Ray finished eating and leaned back on his elbows. The warm midday sun was making him sleepy. Knowing there was much to be done, he fought off the feeling. It was half an hour on that he heard Wally approaching the camp on his dun horse.

'You'll never guess what I found up there,' Wally

called out. Ray got to his feet, almost staggering with sleepiness.

'What?' he shouted back. His eyes through blurry, half-alert vision had already revealed something that made no sense to his sun-numbed brain. He frowned, tried to will himself to complete awareness.

'This!' Wally cried. Now Ray saw that he had not been imagining the dream figure. Wally, sitting his dun, hat tilted back, was holding his lariat in one gloved hand.

The other end of the rope was looped around a desperate-looking Indian woman. She was frail, smudged, frightened. There was blood on the front of the white muslin dress she wore beneath a fringed buckskin jacket.

'Good God, Wally! What have you done?'

'It's called rescue,' Wally Chambers said, swinging down from his horse. 'Don't give that loop around her any thought. She could have thrown it off any time she wanted. It's not drawn tight.'

'Then why didn't she?' Ray asked, meeting the obsidian gaze of the diminutive, dark-skinned woman.

'That's obvious – she didn't want to,' Wally said. He approached the dead camp-fire and nodded his approval at the remaining meal there. 'You done all right, Ray,' Wally, aid, crouching beside the tin plate with the meal intended for him. He still had hold of the rope. Now he beckoned to the girl and she came forward uneasily, but with eager eyes. She, too, squatted near the cold fire. Wally nudged the tin plate nearer to her and made eating motions with his hand. The girl-woman hesitated and then attacked the food with both hands, voraciously shoving the ham, sweet potatoes and biscuits into her mouth, making small animal grunts of satisfaction as she ate. She still wore Wally's loop of rope loosely around her.

'You wouldn't believe what she was doing when I ran across her at the spring – the water source is good and clear, by the way.'

'What was she doing?' Ray asked. He was scowling. The woman looked up at him fearfully, glanced at Wally's smiling face and went back to her greedy eating.

'I swear to you . . . Ray, she was trying to cut a chunk of meat from the haunch of a dead coyote.' He held up the crudest of chipped white stone knives to show Ray. 'And the animal had been dead a day or two.'

No wonder Wally had felt pity for the Indian girl. 'Why the rope?' Ray had to ask.

'Well, she was scared stiff at the sight of me. I tried to beckon to her, using sign language' – Wally smiled – 'even used the five words of Apache language that I learned some years ago. That did nothing to calm her down. She just stood petrified, staring at me. So I took her prisoner.'

'You did, did you?'

'Sure,' Wally said rather proudly. 'That way she didn't have to feel any shame about giving herself up.'

'Why would she. . . ?'

'It's a part of the Indians' way,' Wally told him. 'You don't just give yourself up to an enemy. So I took her prisoner – sort of.'

The girl was now finished eating. She looked around

as if hoping for more, but her face was contented. She sucked at her fingers and readjusted Wally's noose.

'She's not Apache, I don't think,' Ray said.

'No. I don't think so either,' Wally agreed. 'See that necklace she's wearing? All bleached bone. Never seen an Apache woman with something like that, and her dress is wrong for them. What I think she is, is Jumano. There's only two reasons she should be alone up here, Ray – I was thinking this over on the trail down.'

'What two reasons?' Ray asked, as the woman continued to squat near Wally's feet like a faithful hound, her dark eyes softly satisfied.

'She could be a totem squaw,' Wally said, bringing up an unfamiliar term.

'A totem squaw?' Ray said.

'I've heard of the practice,' Wally went on, still smiling at the woman. 'But it seems to be more common up north – among the Utes and other Indians up that way. If the tribe has to leave its land to follow the buffalo herds, or is driven out by hard weather, or an invading tribe, they leave one woman behind to kind of mark their territory. If they come back some day and find the woman still alive, their claim to the land is still good in the eyes of the gods. If she's dead . . . it's a sign they should move on to a newer place.'

Ray slowly digested this as he watched the squatting girl with the enormous black eyes who kept them fixed steadily on Wally Chambers as he was speaking.

'You said you came up with two reasons why she might be up here alone, Wally. What was the second?'

'If she's Jumano – and I think she is – or some

smaller branch of that tribe, I think she might be the last of her people.'

Ray's anger with Wally had faded away. He now only felt pity for the girl without even knowing what sort of deprivations she had endured. She had had water and survived by scavenging, but what kind of life was that for a woman?

'I'm thinking that maybe the Mescaleros wiped her people out – there's no way of knowing, of course,' Wally said. 'But here she is alone and desperate. I couldn't think of anything else to do but bring her back to camp.'

'Wally, you found her, but you can't keep her,' Ray said with a sternness he did not feel, even though it was true. What could they do with a lost Indian woman along the danger trail? They would not be leading her to safety, finding a better life for her, but simply getting her entangled in their own problems. Giving her a meal was one thing, but. . . . The woman's eyes looked up to Ray beseechingly. She had to know that they were discussing what to do with her without even understanding a word of their language. She scooted nearer to Wally as if for protection.

'What's her name?' Ray asked, softening.

'I don't know – is Kata a name? She kept repeating that along the trail. It might mean devil or please or friend or help. I don't know. Kata?' Wally asked, bending down, and the girl's wide eyes brightened. She gripped Wally's leg with both hands and nodded.

'I guess it's Kata,' Wally said.

'That'll have to do for now,' Ray replied. 'But look,

Wally, all of your guesses could be wrong. She could have family around.'

'Leaving her out on her own to live off carrion?'

'All right.' Ray ran a hand across his head. 'Maybe her people have gone but are going to be coming back soon – something delayed them.'

'Like dying,' Wally said. He loosened the girl's fingers from his leg and then took the loop off her small body. That caused her to shudder. Some dogs will quiver if you remove their collars, as if the pack is rejecting them by removing their symbol of belonging. Kata's silently pleading reaction as the lariat was slipped was similar. Was she now being rejected by these strange men?

'Oh, hell,' Ray said in frustration. 'I don't care what you do with her. But there's no way she'll be able to keep up and I won't wait for her along the trail.'

'Ray?' Wally said, coiling his rope again. 'Just thinking – don't you figure old Bess would carry another hundred pounds without much complaint?'

FOUR

Ray wasn't feeling noble as they crossed the creek and moved on into the white mountains, only foolish. He led their small party onward across the barren land. He tried to pay little attention to Kata, who now rode on the back of Bess, seated awkwardly on their food packs. She showed no discomfort, nor did the mule seem troubled by its added burden. Kata actually smiled once as the cheerful Wally Chambers chattered to her.

'I taught her my name,' Wally said brightly as he rode beside Ray. 'What do you think of that?'

There was nothing for Ray to do but provide a positive response to his friend's cheerful message.

His own thoughts were a little deeper and a shade darker. What if Kata somehow managed to get free of them with the mule? If they lost their supplies in this desolate country they would be little better off than the Jumano woman had been when Wally found her.

From time to time as they rode deeper into the unknown territory, Ray thought he glimpsed something, like a faint, moving shadow or a flicker of movement in the rounded white hills that surrounded them. At times, also, he thought he could feel eyes following them – a sensation those who have not had it happen to them would scoff at.

Wally Chambers had similar sensations. They discussed it as they rode side by side across the land, which was now dry and pale beneath the glare of the high sun.

'There's somebody dogging our trail,' Wally said. 'I can feel it, Ray.'

'I have the same feeling. Couldn't be Indians, do you think?'

'Why? Because we've kidnapped a lovely Indian princess?' Wally responded lightly. More seriously he said, 'No, I don't think so. Neither do I think it's Duke. His style would be to ride up to us and order us back to the home ranch.'

'I think you're right,' Ray Hardin said. No, it wasn't Lyle Wycherly's style to ride the high range, simply watching their progress. 'Who, then?'

'It bothers me that these hills are supposed to be rife with outlaws, Ray. They would be on the watch all the time, looking out for lawmen or the army.'

Ray nodded with silent agreement. He had been thinking along those lines himself. 'Well, we're obviously neither of those. We aren't wearing any badges and we aren't dressed in blue. Any watcher must have come to the same conclusion.' Ray glanced at Kata as he did occasionally to make sure the mule was still with them, although with their cow ponies he and Wally could easily run down the slow-plodding Bess if the woman attempted such a trick. He told Wally the thought that had occurred to him earlier.

'If anyone we don't know comes around asking, I think we ought to tell them that we're silver prospectors, searching for a rich vein we've heard about up here.'

'That sounds all right, Ray, but we're not packing any tools.'

'I didn't say we were working, just prospecting.'

'That's going to sound a little flimsy, but I have nothing better to offer,' Wally said. 'Let's just hope no one is bothered enough by us to even ask our business.'

'That's my hope as well, but I have the feeling someone is keeping a close eye on us.'

'Kata?' Wally asked, glancing back. 'How do we explain her?'

'Why would anyone ask about the woman? There's reasons for keeping a squaw with us. She does the cooking and minds the supplies on the pack animal.'

'I guess that'll do,' Wally Chambers agreed. 'She sure won't put the lie to it.' He smiled again then – a weaker expression than usual. 'What are you really thinking about, Ray? Since we are no threat to a band of outlaws, that can't be it. They'd probably be willing to leave us alone to maintain their secrets.'

'All right,' Ray Hardin replied after a long silence, as the horses plodded on, 'it's this that's bothering me more: what is Lyle Wycherly doing up here at all? And it has to be him, because as you pointed out there is nothing at the end of the western trail but the Broken W, and he is the one who tried to warn us off. Why?

'It's to his benefit as much as anyone else's if we can

find a shorter route through to Fort Davis, yet he seemed intent on disrupting the plan before we could even get started up the trail.'

Wally, who had been meditative, said, 'Something to do with the outlaws?'

'The story you were telling about the Blue Moon-KL affair got me to thinking.'

'You mean you think Lyle wants the Broken W Ranch?'

'And he wants it now! Maybe . . . I don't know, Wally. I'm still trying to think it through. It could be that I'm letting my personal dislike of Lyle Wycherly color my thoughts.'

'Duke Wycherly isn't an easy man to like,' Wally agreed. 'But if you're right, what would be the point in all of this?'

'It could be – if Lyle is involved in shady business – that he was the one tipping off the rustlers and highwaymen when a herd was coming through along the south trail, taking a cut of his own from the proceeds. If Glen Wycherly decided on a new route to follow to Fort Davis, Lyle's accomplices would have to be notified so as not to send out an ambush party when the steers were not going to be driven that way at all.'

'I guess that makes sense,' Wally agreed. 'But if there is an outlaw town up here, old man Wycherly will be delivering the beeves to their doorstep for them. Broken W has some good hands, some tough men, but they're not up to battling an army of outlaws, I don't think.

'Ray,' Wally continued, 'if what you're thinking is

true, maybe it would be better for all concerned if we just gave it up right now – returned to the Broken W and told Glen Wycherly that we could not find a decent trail through the Poconos.'

'Because we suspect his son is a thief?'

'I know it's only suspicion, but I'd hate to see our boys get tangled up in a gun battle because of us.'

'So would I, Wally, and that's a fact,' Ray answered, 'but you're forgetting something: we ride for the brand and we've been given a job to do. The decision is Glen Wycherly's. We'll tell him what we suspect even if it rubs him the wrong way. After that, it's still his ranch and his decision to make.' They spoke no more about it.

Ray knew that this day would be longer, slower, than those previously, studying the land falls and trying to sketch them out with his untrained eye and hand. They had to backtrack once from a three-mile trek into what proved to be a box canyon. Everything was slow progress. Ray called frequent halts as he swung down and crudely mapped the land. Once Kata approached him at his work and stood silent and apparently confused at what he was trying to do with his chicken-scratches. She didn't seem to grasp the connection between the land around her and Ray's drawings. That could have been partly due to his lack of expertise.

In the middle of the afternoon, Ray folded the map and tucked it away again. He thought he was getting better at knolls. From the ground Wally, seated beside the patient Kata, was watching.

'Have you thought about us finding a campsite yet?'

Wally Chambers asked.

'There's still plenty of daylight left,' Ray said, glancing at the slanting sun, 'but if you happen to spot a place, preferably with some shade, we'll make an early camp.' Ray wouldn't have admitted it, but he was tired already. This seemed to be an endless journey to nowhere. Maybe Wally was right: they should just pull off and return to the Broken W. Kata looked up at him, expecting nothing. She seemed to be content as long as Wally was nearby. How long could that last, Ray wondered? Chambers would have to make a decision soon as to what he intended to do with the Jumano girl. That was one question Ray refused to involve himself in. He had conflicting feelings about the matter.

She looked a little more content than she had when Wally had brought her into their camp, but her relief was only the result of being saved from a desperate situation. How long could Wally be expected to play savior? They came from two very different worlds.

Now Kata continued to study Ray, wondering what advice or command he would give his friend, since she had accepted Ray as the tribal leader. Her clothing was still filthy. Ray wondered if it had once been her best costume. Her face remained smudged, her straight, blue-black hair snarled. A woman whose people had abandoned her and whom time had forgotten.

It was too much to ponder at that moment when Ray needed to be thinking of so many other things.

Judging that it was time to be moving – sitting there would do nothing to advance their cause – Ray started back toward his tri-colored paint pony.

And a bullet winged past him and sent up a puff of dust a bare fraction of a second before the distinctive bark of a Winchester rifle echoed down the hills.

Ray Hardin had the time to slip his own rifle from its scabbard and roll to the ground behind his horse, which was not startled by the distant shot. Taking a position on one knee, Ray scanned the convoluted white hills above them, seeing nothing. Wally had Kata pressed to the earth beneath him, his Colt in his hand. His questioning eyes flickered to Ray.

'What was that?' Wally asked in a low-voiced whisper.

'A warning,' Ray hissed back. 'Nothing more. A decent marksman could have plugged either of us, even at that distance.'

'What follows the first warning?' Wally said. 'A second?'

'Maybe that was the first and final warning,' Ray said. 'Want to turn back, Wally?'

'Hell, no! They've gotten me mad now. That bullet might have hit Kata, and after all she's been through just trying to survive!'

Despite the tenseness of the moment, Ray had to smile. Wally was taking his stewardship seriously. Or was it more than that? It seemed improbable, but there was never any telling in these matters.

'There's a small notch in the hills ahead that I saw earlier,' Wally said. 'It might make a decent campsite, if you think it might be time to fort up for the night.'

'I think it might be,' Ray said, rising to dust off. 'Wally, would you get off that woman now?'

With blustering, embarrassed denials, Wally Chambers

got to his feet as well, leaving a perplexed Kata on the ground, looking up at the two of them. Ray watched, trying to conceal his smile.

'This campsite you found, Wally, is there any water up there?'

'I didn't see so much as a trickle, though there's a few oaks growing there. Why do you ask? We've got plenty of water in those kegs.'

'I'd hate to use enough of that for a full-out bath,' Ray said, swinging into the saddle of his patient pony.

'Are you crazy, Ray? Another bath? Ever since Miss Patricia gave you that soap and a toothbrush, you've thought of nothing but scrubbing yourself up.'

Ray ignored the implication and said to Wally, who was now beside him mounted on his dun horse, 'I wasn't thinking of myself.' He nodded in the direction of Kata, who was on top of Bess again. 'Getting cleaned up might make her feel better about herself.'

'She seems to feel fine,' Wally said. 'She probably don't even know what soap is.'

'Of course she does,' Ray said, wondering at Wally's balkiness. 'All of the local tribes have been using yarrow-root soap for hundreds of years or more. She just hasn't had anything to wash up with lately. She's a woman; she deserves to be clean. Of course we could take the time to stop and build a sweat lodge.'

'I yield,' Wally said with a grin. 'We'll rig something up so she can use the water from one of the casks.'

'Good idea. You wait and see, she'll be much happier.'

Wally's grin faded. 'Ray, you're not getting any ideas

about cleaning me up as well, are you?'

'That's between you and her,' Ray said, starting his pony. It felt good to give a little of Wally's needling back to him.

The camp, when they reached it, was not badly situated. Atop a low, featureless outcropping, four dusty-appearing live oaks stood, casting their thin shade. It was a secure position, which was what they had been concerned about finding after the sniper – whoever it was – had loosed that shot in their direction.

No one could possibly have scaled the bluff opposite to try to pick a target. No one could enter the concealed notch without being seen. It was safe enough for now.

Together Ray and Wally Chambers unburdened Bess of her load. Kata made herself useful by placing the goods in an orderly arrangement to one side. Ray hated to see the deprived Jumano woman working so hard, but he understood: she needed to feel useful, to earn her keep. Later Ray and Wally toted one of the heavy casks beyond the trees where they found a convenient ledge five feet off the ground. They wedged the cask there. Standing back, hands on hips, Ray took a few deep breaths. He hated using their precious water in this way, but after all it had been his idea.

'I just hope she doesn't waste any of it,' he said to Wally.

'She won't,' Wally answered confidently.

He was probably right: this was a land where water was valued and used sparingly for drinking, cooking or bathing. Certainly Kata was aware of their present situation although she could not tell them as much. Back in the camp Ray dug through his saddle-bags, removing the block of yellow lye soap. He tossed it to Wally, saying, 'You explain it to her.'

'She'll get the idea when I show her the keg and the soap,' Wally replied. That the cowhand was getting strongly attached to the Indian woman was obvious. Ray could only hope that it did not lead to more problems. They already had all that they could handle. . . .

The chief of which was Lyle Wycherly. Where was the strutting young man, and what did he have in mind? What was he even doing in the remote Poconos? Ray unsaddled his horse, gave each of the animals something to drink from the bucket and propped himself up in the shade cast by the fronting bluff, thinking.

He came to no conclusions as the sun sank behind the jutting bluff and the shadows deepened. A breeze, arriving with the settling of evening, rattled the leaves of the live-oak trees. Ray dozed in the coolness of the pre-sundown hour.

He was startled awake, but saw no cause for his sudden waking. Wally had started a small camp-fire, and, bless him, had done some cooking while Ray slept. Ray rose slowly, stretching his limbs. The scent of coffee was in the air and that of fried ham. He almost wished that he had let Wally bring the dried beans and other supplies he had wanted to. Ray liked smoked ham well enough, but not at every meal.

'What's for supper?' he asked, as he reached the camp-fire.

'What you see,' Wally answered with a smile. He was

crouched over the fire. Kata sat on a nearby white rock, her hands folded on her lap. Her long hair looked glossy in the firelight. Her face was no longer smudged. Her white dress seemed to be cleaner. How much water had she used? Ray hoped he did not come to regret his decision. But Kata looked happy, content, so for the moment all was well in the camp.

'There's ham, and I still have some of those salt biscuits we pinched from the cook's supply,' Wally told him. 'And some greens I'm boiling.'

'What kind of greens?'

'Well, I think they're mustard greens, but maybe not,' Wally said. 'Kata went out and gathered them while you were sleeping the afternoon away. And she should know what she's doing. She's been living off the wild-growing things for a long time.'

'It'll do,' Ray said. He was still a little grumpy after his uncomfortable nap. He sagged to a seating position on the ground, wrinkled his nose and looked at Wally. 'Is that by any chance lye soap that I smell on you, Wally?'

The fire-flush on Wally's face deepened. 'Ah, Ray, don't go on about that, please.' He handed him a tin plate and poured a cup of coffee for himself, going to sit beside Kata as the fire flickered low and dusk settled.

They decided to picket the stock farther away from where they meant to sleep. Too much can go wrong with horses and men in close proximity when the animals are dozing as well. Startled awake by some large desert creature or a sudden noise, they could take to their heels without noticing their nearby sleeping masters. Kata, of course, would be sleeping away from the men as well. She was capable of finding her own spot to bed down.

The fire extinguished itself and the stars began to flicker on in brilliant clusters across the sky. The moon would not be rising for another hour or so to illuminate the barren land. Kata and Wally had gone to their separate beds to roll up in their blankets, anticipating the cold night to follow the bright day. Ray Hardin sat up for awhile, blanket over his shoulders as he tried once again to work his way through the puzzle that this journey had become.

He had no luck with that except to make himself more certain than ever that Lyle Wycherly held the key to events. And where was Wycherly on this night? He was not the sort of man who stoically endures rough camping.

Giving it up, Ray decided events would just have to play themselves out. He was not going to think his way through this maze on this night, and there was a deal of hard travelling to do in the morning. As he was preparing to roll up in his own bed, he saw – just for a moment – the distant, wavering flicker of a light across the long distances to the east. The camp-fire of some lonely prospector or an equally reclusive Indian?

It seemed not, but there was no telling. The light shimmered through the atmosphere disturbed and bent by rising heatwaves as the earth released its warmth to the skies, and then seemed to vanish.

Ray shrugged and then put his head down. He had

decided that there was no point in dwelling on questions that could not be solved.

FIVE

Morning was cool; a dark sky shot through with orange clung to the eastern horizon. Ray Hardin awakened stiffly after the chill of night, summoned back to alertness by the hand of Wally Chambers shaking his shoulder, and his urgent voice.

'She's gone, Ray!' Wally, who had not so much as planted his hat over his disarranged blond hair, said with anger, sorrow and surprise all mingled on his face and in his tone of voice. 'Kata's gone – and she's taken Bess and all our supplies.'

'That leaves us in a mess, doesn't it?' said Ray, sitting up and reaching for his own Stetson. He had feared something like this from the beginning. Now, it seemed, it had happened. 'When?' he asked the distraught Wally.

'How would I know?' Wally answered, waving his hands around. 'Sometime in the middle of the night. 'Why, Ray? Why would she do that to us?'

'We had some things she needed, that's why. If she is supposed to be the one watching over her tribe's homeland – a totem squaw – she saw the chance to make survival more bearable as she waits for their return.'

'But. . . .' Wally was sputtering as he talked, obviously confused by events. 'We took her in, fed her when she had nothing to eat. I thought she was becoming my friend. . . .'

And more? Ray wondered, without asking aloud.

'Look, Wally,' he said, placing a hand on his friend's shoulder, 'Kata comes from a different world with different beliefs, different ways of looking at life, different precepts. It may be that she believed her chief obligation is to her people, not to two passing strangers.'

'I can see that,' Wally mumbled, turning away, 'but how could she have done this to me!' He struck a fist against his palm and stood looking out at the barren land, hands on his hips.

Ray Hardin reminded him, 'We can't go chasing after her. We need that mule and the supplies, yes, but could we ever catch her here – in this land she was brought up on? It seems unlikely and, besides, we'd be wasting a lot of time while Glen Wycherly is desperate for our report. We have our obligations, too, Wally.'

'Oh, hell,' Wally answered, 'I know all of that. But. . . .' There was a notable shadow of discouragement in his voice. His gaze returned from the distances to meet Ray's eyes. 'What are we supposed to do now, Ray? Without supplies and a pack animal?'

'Continue,' Ray said almost cheerfully, although he was feeling far from cheerful, 'and be glad she didn't have the chance to gather our riding stock.'

'We won't make it far or fast without supplies.'

'No, we won't,' Ray had to agree.

Ray Hardin was saddling his paint horse, drawing the twin cinches tight. The morning sun had already ridden high enough that Ray had tugged his hat down against its glare. 'Any water left in that bathing keg we put on that ledge yesterday?'

'There should be, yes.'

'Let's give it to the ponies now, then. We've still got our canteens. Mine are both almost full.'

'That's fine for a while,' Wally said, determined to continue to complain – maybe he had the right. A little of his faith in his fellow man – or woman – had been shattered. 'What are we going to do in the long run, Ray? We can't go out hunting. If there is any game in these godforsaken hills, we don't even know where they go to drink, and we have to find something to eat.'

'I've an idea,' Ray said, 'but I don't think you'll like it much – I know I don't.'

'Try it on me,' Wally said, swinging the saddle onto his dun horse's back. 'Any idea is welcome.'

'I think there's a town ahead,' Ray told him. 'I saw a light last night where none belongs.'

'A town?' Wally asked, scoffing. 'There's nothing up in these hills, or we would have heard about it . . . unless it's an outlaw town.'

'It could very well be,' Ray said. 'But then, outlaws have to eat, too. There will be supplies of some kind there.'

'And a bunch of bad-tempered types with a lot of guns.'

'Why would they want to bother with two wandering silver prospectors?' Ray asked. 'We can grab a sack of flour, some dry beans and a side of bacon before anyone even knows we were there.'

'And a pack animal,' Ray suggested.

'And a pack animal. Outlaws are seldom short on horses as they are necessary to their business.'

'You're saying we should voluntarily ride into an outlaw town?'

'I'm saying that we do that or learn to eat sand,' Ray said, his smile completely absent now.

What had happened to Kata was that the small sounds in the night had awakened her to the movements of a stranger, poorly illuminated by the rising moon. White man, red man? She could not even tell that much in the shadowed oak grove. She did not see the distinctive wide-brimmed hat that white riders always wore, but that meant nothing, He could have lost his hat or placed it temporarily aside in the night while he went about his work.

Which was stealing the mule and their food supplies. Bess shuffled her feet as if in annoyance, but made little sound. Her shod hoofs had been muffled, perhaps with soft leather socks. That was a trick of the Apache horse-thieves, but any man could have learned it. She watched the stealthy man shadowing his way through the trees. She knew what he was up to, but she remained still, afraid to call out.

If the two men she was traveling with were to awaken from deep sleep, wrapped up in their blankets, they would scramble for their weapons. The intruder was already awake and ready. Two sleep-glazed men would be able to provide little opposition. Probably they would be killed in their beds if they tried to react.

That left it up to Kata, who was alert and ready. She saw that the man had already thrown the bulk of their goods over the mule's back, moving silently and without haste. He walked away from the sleeping men, coming so close to Kata that he thought she would see her. But she was small, the shadows deep, and his eyes were only on the two men.

Now what?

Kata rose from her bed in the chill of night. There was the slightest of night breezes drifting down the canyon. The man passed by her and led the silently rigged Bess out toward the open land. Kata left her blanket and her jacket behind as she started after the intruder. She carried only determination and the flaked white-stone knife she held clenched in her small hand.

She did not have to guess which way the man was going. She had known this country since childhood. He would take the long trail which wound higher onto the bluff and then sloped down to the flats. This was the only way out of the canyon except the way their party had entered, and the stranger would not want to risk the sleeping men being awakened by some sound and mounting their horses to follow him. Kata followed the silent man and silent mule along the rough, winding, moon-illuminated trail.

She would jog along, then slow to a walk to breathe. She knew Bess's pace well enough and knew that she was capable of running them down. She knew there was a switchback in the trail ahead where it dipped into darkness before rising into the blue moonlight again, and Kata glanced up the rocky slope.

She could do it. She tucked her knife into the woven belt she wore and began to scramble upward. No mule could have gone this way, but Kata could. Panting, straining, she reached the trail. There was still no sign of man or mule, but they would have to pass this way. There was no other way out of the hills. Kata paused, saw a group of boulders and slipped behind them, merging her shadow with theirs.

She waited, listening, trying to still her labored breath. She was young, she was physically strong despite the deprivations of recent weeks, but the excitement of the night seemed to have stifled her breathing, raised her heart rate. No matter, she would do what must be done. She was proud; she would fight. For she now owed her debt of allegiance to Wall-ee and his chief.

The muffled clopping of the mule's hoofs was plain enough in the night as the thief made his way down the trail. Kata waited, crouched behind the stack of boulders, her breath coming in tight little gasps, her stone knife clenched tightly in her hand.

The angular, shadowed figure of a man leading Bess appeared on the moonlit road, moving away from the darkness beyond. He must have thought that his thievery was now successfully completed. He moved in a shambling, loose-gaited way. Bess followed, her head bowed with the inevitably of the life of a beast of burden.

Now Kata could hear the man's footsteps though he was wearing moccasins or very soft-soled shoes. The man, whoever he was, must have been counting himself lucky on this night.

But this was the night he was to die.

When the man's tall figure showed itself around the shoulder of the concealing rocks, Kata sprang forward. Bess reared in startlement and Kata could hear the hastily packed supplies the mule carried tumble away into the depths of the canyon. But she had her eyes fixed only on the tall man who whirled toward her in surprise, his arm uplifted in a fending position. Kata's knife blade struck below the upraised arm, and the point of it drove deeply into the man's chest.

The dark man grabbed Kata with both arms. He was immensely strong. He lifted her from the ground, shaking her like a mother bear with a mutinous cub. But the strength of his arms was not enough. The struggling Kata could feel the breath trickling out of her body. The images before her eyes began to swirl and fade and there was a deepening blackness about the sky. But blood was flowing from her attacker's mouth now. Dark in the night, it flowed down his face and onto his clothes and hers. His strength was ebbing. There was a quivering in his body, arms and legs. His grip suddenly loosened and he fell back against the earth. Kata knew he was dead.

She sat on the cold earth beside the dead man, her legs drawn up, arms looped around them, waiting for her vision to clear, for her breathing to return to normal.

Kata felt tired, very tired suddenly. When she tried to rise, her knees trembled and then buckled beneath her.

She could not go on yet. Bess had returned to stand near her, a puzzled, equine look in her eyes. Kata knew that she must rise, return the mule to the camp. Wall-ee would expect it of her. She expected it of herself.

She tried to rise again, could not, and toppled onto her side to fall asleep on this dark, lonely trail in the chill of night.

Ray Hardin and Wally Chambers rode on toward where they now suspected the outlaw town lay. It was probably the worst idea Hardin had ever had in his life, Wally reflected, but what else were they to do? They no longer remotely resembled prospectors. Without the pack mule, wearing their cowboy gear and sitting cow ponies, they looked exactly like what they were – two rambling cowhands. Ray had suggested the somewhat shaky tale that they had been fired off the ranch they were working on and decided to drift this way on a whim. Wally didn't like the feel of it, but he had nothing better to suggest.

It was true they had nothing much the outlaws could want – except their horses – but men had been killed over a horse before now. The outlaws – reputed to be the Jack 'Blue Moon' Priest's gang – might assume that these uninvited snoopers had been sent to scout out their robbers' stronghold by someone. The suspicion alone was enough to get them murdered. This was a rough crowd and known to be quite sudden in their decisions.

And what of Lyle Wycherly? If their suspicions were correct, Duke must have ridden this way himself. The moment the rancher's son laid eyes on them he could put the lie to any story they had concocted.

All of this was troubling the small blond cowhand only distantly as they rode on across the flats toward their uncertain destiny. His mind was fixed on only one gloomy, clinging thought: a woman's perfidy.

A man's mind can work that way where women are concerned.

They had rescued Kata, fed her, bathed her, befriended her. How could she have just turned her back on them, stolen from them, slipped away in the night? But she had. Wally decided he had better do some long thinking about the way he had regarded women and the treacherous human race as a whole.

'There's someone coming up behind us,' Ray Hardin said, interrupting Wally's brooding thoughts. 'And it looks like they're trying to catch up.'

'Can you tell who it is?' Wally asked.

'Not at this distance, but I make it out to be only one rider. Why don't we pull up and see who it is? I'd grab my rifle while we wait if I were you.'

Wally Chambers nodded, slowed his dun horse and then halted it as he unsheathed his Winchester. They squinted into the sun and watched the approaching figure through the rising heat veils, muscles tensed, rifles tightly gripped, until Ray relaxed and lowered his Winchester. He could now see that the animal was Bess the mule, and the rider was a woman in a white costume. He told Wally, 'You can lower your weapon, you won't need it. It's Kata riding Bess.'

'What's she doing here?' Wally growled.

'Trying to catch up, it seems.'

Wally Chambers continued to scowl as he lowered his rifle and stood watching, waiting for the rider to reach them. He had built up an anger and was reluctant to let go of it. 'There aren't any provisions on that mule,' he said to Ray.

'Something must have happened.'

'You're right, something happened! She took off with the mule and stashed the provisions somewhere for her own use.'

'We can't know that, Wally.'

'You explain it, then,' Chambers said with some heat.

'I can't because I just don't know; maybe we never will know.'

Kata was now only twenty yards or so from them. Her face looked grim, cheerful at the same time. Her bright eyes were fixed on Chambers. She waved a hand.

'Wall-ee!'

'You *did* teach her your name,' Ray said, swinging from his horse's saddle to stand beside the glaring Wally Chambers.

'Yeah, just don't ask me why I bothered.'

'Back off a bit, Wally – we don't know what happened to the girl.'

'Here she is with our mule,' Wally said, not pacified.

'Here she is when she could be dozens of other places,' Ray said.

As he spoke Kata was slipping from the back of Bess. She started to rush toward Wally and then broke her stride, perhaps seeing the anger darkening his face. Her head lowered and she approached with a shuffling gait, hands behind her back. She stood in front of Wally

Chambers like an accused prisoner and then began talking rapidly, eagerly, in a language neither man understood. She made hand gestures, waved to the far distance, at Bess, and then stood quietly, waiting for the verdict.

'What did she say?' Ray asked in a low voice.

'How the hell should I know?' Wally shot back, His tone was enough to cause Kata to back away a few steps, her wide eyes pleading for forgiveness or understanding – there was no telling which.

'There's blood on the front of her dress,' Ray Hardin pointed out. 'She's been through some trouble.' Wally remained silent, his expression unforgiving.

'I think we'd better believe her.'

'Believe what?' Wally said, turning toward Ray. 'I don't speak her language. All I can believe is what I know: she took off with our mule and supplies. The supplies are gone.'

'She wouldn't have come back if she were guilty, Wally. Something happened last night, and we haven't an idea what it is.'

'I have an idea,' Wally said with bitterness.

'I have an idea, too,' Ray Hardin said carefully. 'You felt betrayed, and you had the right – if things were as you suspected. Well, now Kata is back. She has a tale to tell us that we can't understand. That has to be frustrating for her.

'I think you should just trust her, Wally. I think you have to trust her or you'll never be able to trust anyone again as long as you live.'

'That's the way you feel about it, is it, Ray?'

'That's the way I feel about it.'

'Well. . . .' Wally Chambers removed his hat, put it back on and shuffled a foot. 'All right. I'll do it for you, Ray.'

'You're not understanding what I'm saying, Wally – do it for yourself.'

With the uncertain Kata again mounted on Bess, they started along their way. It was a silent, sullen group. Yet by the time they had gone a few miles, Wally had dropped back a bit to ride beside Kata. The relief on her face was obvious, and once Ray even glimpsed the flicker of a smile on her pretty face.

Ahead now the land remained flat, the trail wide enough for any herd to travel. The white hills were lower here, bunched together like neglected children. There was an occasional group of oak trees, with here and there a ragged cottonwood tree. There were clumps of nopal cactus and much greasewood dotted the land. It was not an unpleasant scene and the day was cooling as the sun wheeled over toward the distant western horizon, sending long shadows out before their horses.

And ahead, somewhere – not far along now – was Blue Moon Priest's outlaw camp where there would be hell to pay if the men there did not like their looks.

SIX

'There it is,' Ray Hardin said, pointing out the collection of shacks ahead of them. The town wasn't really even that. It was a group of formless, sagging structures clustered together among the house-sized red boulders. Whatever they could scavenge or loot had been tacked together for shelter and commerce – whatever that might consist of. But, there would be some sort of food supplies there, had to be. Even the paltriest town needed food and water to survive.

'What are we supposed to be?' Wally Chambers asked.

'We're back to being prospectors, I suppose. With Kata and the mule we look more the part.'

'What happened is, we were raided by Indians and they took our tools and grub?'

'I suppose so, if anyone asks.'

'All right. Tell me, Ray, have we any money to purchase supplies?'

'Glen Wycherly gave me a little, though I told him I didn't see where we could spend it. He said, no matter, a man should never walk around naked.'

'I hope it isn't too much money,' Wally said without cheer. 'In a place like this more than a few silver dollars would draw a crowd.'

'I know – tell me, what's really bothering you, Wally?' Ray Hardin asked, seeing uneasiness in his young friend's eyes. Wally glanced behind them.

'Kata,' Wally admitted with a small sigh. 'What are we leading her into? You know, Ray, if there's one thing in short supply up here, it'll be women.'

'We'll stay wary. If need be, we'll hie out of here without supplies and see how good we really are at roughing it. That is,' Ray added, 'if we can find a way out. The outlaws are using some kind of trail, but it may be hidden among the rocks, wide enough for only a single horse at a time. I doubt it's large enough for a herd of cattle.' Ray was still thinking about his primary purpose in being in the Poconos, to find a way the Broken W herd could be driven through to Fort Davis.

'They'll likely have lookouts posted along it,' Wally thought. 'Blue Moon didn't get as far as he has by being careless. If the army finds that trail, it'd be like someone having left the back door open.'

'You're right, though we've heard nothing about the army being out looking for Blue Moon.'

'Out where we are, we don't hear much,' Wally replied. 'Anyway, let's do what we came to do and get out of here as quickly as we can. Maybe someone will be happy to point us on our way just to get rid of us.'

Ray slowed his paint pony even more. They had reached the outskirts of the ramshackle town. He let his eyes flicker to the heights of the huge red rocks, looking for watching men. Wally was right – the outlaws would never relax their vigilance. They could not afford to. Probably their approach had already been noted and reported.

Wally, he noticed, had turned up the brim of his hat in front. Ray frowned a question at the blond kid.

'It's the way I always imagine a prospector looking,' Wally hissed.

Ray shrugged. It was a mighty thin disguise. Kata rode behind on the placid mule. Neither showed any signs of agitation. Perhaps Kata thought in her ignorance and out of blind faith that the two men must know what they were doing. Nothing could be further from the truth. It would have been nice to somehow give the girl a word or two of caution, but such was not possible.

They were now among the shanties of the town, thrown together on the side of a curving, dusty street. Out of habit Ray glanced at the front of the structures. He realized it was futile. A band of wild-country outlaws do not paint the names of their establishments on buildings. Two of the places they had so far passed were obviously drinking places – they were not even grand enough to be called frontier saloons. Just shacks where the liquor was stored.

The first man they passed on the sun-bleached street was of middle age, dressed in a blue cavalry shirt and black jeans. He wore a red scarf around his neck. His eyebrows were a curious white with tufts of hair jutting up and out from them. He wore his Colt revolver low.

He watched them in passing, nodded to himself as if in satisfaction and turned away up a trash-strewn alley.

Now they know we're here, Ray thought as he continued to look around. The town was slovenly as well as being rickety and shabby. A temporary sanctuary built to be abandoned at any moment. There was not the slightest hint of civic pride about it. It was as disposable as their own lives.

Ray had been watching for any sign of Lyle Wycherly as well. His horse, and those of Sully Parker and Brian Akers. Of course even spotting the animals would mean little. For all they knew Lyle Wycherly was overestimating his standing with the outlaws. Horses could be easily taken from dead men, and if Wycherly had nothing else to offer Blue Moon, then a horse or two would do.

Ray glanced at Wally, whose expression said, 'Whatever we're going to do, let's do it and get out of here.' There was a menace about the place, heavy and oppressive.

'There,' Wally said aloud. He lifted himself a little in the stirrups and pointed to a low, sagging building where someone could be seen unloading a sack of grain from a dilapidated wagon. Ray nodded. It was worth trying. They had to try somewhere.

Riding directly to what they took for a storehouse, for certainly there were no merchants in this town, they halted their ponies. There was no refinement like hitch rails in this place of bandits whose only form of work was performed with six-guns, so Ray simply swung down, handed the reins of his paint pony to Wally and told him, 'I'll see what I can do. Keep your eyes open.'

'You don't think I have been!' Wally said. 'Whatever you do, do it quick, Ray. I want to get Kata out of here.'

They had seen no gathering men, gunhands or otherwise, but now that they had been seen, but not identified, the outlaws would grow dangerously curious. Especially about Kata.

There was no door hung on the entrance to the warehouse. Ray ducked through the doorway and into the interior of the low-roofed, sun-heated building and looked around, waiting for his eyes to adjust to the nearly complete darkness. He could hear men moving around, muttering, smell corn dust and meat which had not been salted down or smoke-treated and was rapidly going bad in the heat.

The man who came forward from the darkness to greet Ray Hardin wore a striped blue vest and trousers; he was coatless in this heat. He had one blind white eye, dark hair parted in the middle, and swollen pink lips. He wore twin walnut-handled Colts. Not your typical storekeeper. However, his voice was not unkind as he asked, 'How can I help you?'

Ray told him the thin fabrication of being two prospectors lost and out of supplies. The man nodded thoughtfully. His expression gave nothing away although he had taken in Ray's wide-brimmed, formed Stetson, the pistol on his hip and pointed-toed boots.

'Let's see what we can do. Have a few dollars, do you?'

'A few,' Ray acknowledged.

'Well, then,' the one-eyed man said, starting away. 'You lost all your goods, that means you don't even have any sacks or burlap bags to carry your goods in, right?

Well, we've got plenty. Now then, follow me through to the back and let's see what we can do for you.'

'Corn meal is stacked over there,' the stranger said, gesturing widely. 'Five-, ten-, twenty-pound sacks. I've got a few sides of bacon over here.' He walked a little farther away and Ray followed.

That was where they jumped him. Ray knew that he should have been expecting something like this, but he had allowed himself to be lulled into a false sense of security by the storeman's affable manner. From behind sacks of flour stacked nearly to the ceiling of the low building, three men emerged.

None of them had friendly intentions.

Ray's hand dropped reflexively toward his holstered Colt, but he found his arms suddenly pinned by yet another man who had managed to slip up behind him. With Ray caught in the man's grip, the first attacker came at him with a short, lethal-looking club.

Ray rocked back against the man who was holding him and lifted both boots to kick out at the man with the club. His heels caught the man high on the chest and he grunted with pain and turned away. The others moved in inexorably, swarming over Ray.

Heavy fists, thrown with savage intent, caught Ray Hardin in the ribs, on the arms, stomach, on his face, which he could not swivel away despite his desperate twisting. A fist caught him on the liver with stunning force, another seemingly carved from granite struck the side of his face below his ear and Ray's head began to ring. There was a slowly descending darkness surrounding him in the dusty confines of the warehouse.

He was aware still of the men beating him, but no longer felt the impact of their blows. There was one last, telling blow delivered against the hinge of his jaw, and then there was nothing but silent darkness as Ray slid free of his attacker's grip and sagged to the floor of the building.

Someone was slapping him, quite hard. In Ray's barely conscious mind it occurred to him that there was an irony in beating a man down with fists and then trying to revive him with more punishment. He tried to open puffed eyes, but could not quite yet. He knew that he was seated in a wooden chair, and tied there more tightly than seemed necessary – he was going nowhere.

'Hit him with some more water,' an unidentifiable voice said from somewhere in the distance.

Ray realized then that he was already soaked through – shirt and trousers were sodden and cold against his flesh. His hair hung damply from his scalp, draping his eyes. Footsteps approached behind him and a bucketful of cold water was dumped onto his head to flow down across his already chilled body.

Ray shivered, realized that meant that he was coming alert, back to life, and pried his eyes open to take in what he could see of the room where he was being held captive.

'That's brought him around,' a man's deep voice said with an unpleasant chuckle. 'Want to get the boss now? He wants to talk to him.'

'Give it awhile,' another man said. 'Right now all he'd be likely to get from our cowboy friend is a gurgling and a babbling. You boys almost did too good a job on him.'

'What'd you expect? The bastard kicked me hard enough to about stop my heart,' a third man complained.

'Hell, everyone knows you got no heart, Artie,' someone gibed.

'Shut up, Sonny! What about you?'

'I did have a heart, but I left it in Abilene,' the man called Sonny answered.

The conversation meant nothing to Ray, and none of it was for his benefit anyway. What mattered was trying to find a way to get free of these thugs. That seemed impossible in a closed room surrounded by four gunmen. He gave up the idea for the time being and let his thoughts, murky and confused as they still were from the beating, drift in other directions.

Who was the boss they had mentioned – the one who wanted to talk to Ray? It had to be Blue Moon Priest, did it not? Or maybe. . . . Ray had a flurry of brief, confused thoughts that failed to connect in his swirling mind. What if the boss was Lyle Wycherly? Perhaps the inadequate popinjay he knew back on the Broken W was only a pose for a cold-blooded gang leader and killer, utilized to throw suspicion from him. Unlikely, but. . . .

Where were Wally and Kata? Perhaps Wally had heard or seen something suspicious at the storehouse and hightailed it out of town with Kata. This seemed less likely than that they also had been taken prisoner and were now being held in a different part of town. Ray regretted dragging Kata into this. He regretted bringing his friend Wally into it. No point in thinking on that – what had been done was done.

Through half-closed eyelids he tried to make out the faces of his abductors. It would do him no good to know their faces now, but who knew, there might come another time on another trail where he would meet up with one of them. Ray Hardin owed each man a debt of revenge.

The huge-shouldered, bulky one was the man named Sonny. The narrow outlaw with the savagely scarred face was the one they had called Artie. The others seemed to have slipped away, probably to celebrate with a few glasses of whiskey. Or, they might have departed out of simple boredom. There's not much entertainment to be had in watching a beaten man strapped to a chair slowly regain consciousness.

'Here he is,' one of them – Artie – said, walking to the flimsy, poorly hung door.

Ray's eyes shifted that way. He had never seen Blue Moon Priest, but from the deferential way these hardcases acted when the big man entered the room, this had to be him. He wore a brown town suit with a glaring red tie held in place by a diamond stickpin. There was a wide smile across his tanned, square face. His hair was black with touches of silver, brushed back severely. Blue Moon Priest looked more like a flashy gambler or a hand-clasping politician than the leader of the most feared outlaw band in the area.

It was the smile, Ray had decided. There was nothing foxy or sham about the expression. It was quite genuine. Most would-be leaders in his profession tried to intimidate by glowering, barking, threatening. Jack Priest somehow managed to dominate without any of these devices. He was a different sort of man. Ray Hardin was about to find out how different Blue Moon was from other common thugs.

'Well, this is him, I suppose,' Priest said, nodding toward Ray, who still sat strapped into the wooden chair. 'You boys might as well go along and have a few drinks.'

'Yeah, thanks, boss,' the big man, Sonny, replied, apparently having no doubt that Blue Moon could take care of business by himself.

The flimsy door swung open on the bright sunlight outside and then flipped shut again.

The boss seated himself on a corner of a wooden table in the corner of the room, eyes and fixed smile beaming in Ray's direction. A long minute dragged by before Priest spoke. Ray watched the dust motes in the beam of sunlight filtering through the half-curtained window. He thought if he looked hard enough he could find some pattern in the way they circled and drifted. He could not. He realized that his thinking was still affected by the beating he had taken. He shook his head, but it did nothing to clear his mind.

'Mister Hardin,' Blue Moon Priest said heartily, as if greeting an old friend, 'my name is Jack Priest. I won't say I'm glad to see you because I'm not. You have come bearing problems.'

'What sort of problems?' Ray asked, although he had already guessed Priest's meaning.

'I do know why you're here,' Priest said, drawing a thin black cigar from his coat's inside pocket and deliberately striking a match on the table top. As he lit it, smoke rose into the sunbeam. Ray could find no pattern in the weave and twist of the silver-blue smoke either. He could not let this game drag out – let's just get it over with. 'Not for supplies,' Blue Moon said.

'We need supplies. Ours got taken.' Ray's head began to thrum and ache dully at the base of his neck. 'There was no place else to go.'

'But that's not all of it,' Priest said, studying the gray ash on the end of his cigar with apparent satisfaction.

'All right,' Ray said, giving in. 'I suppose you must have talked with Lyle Wycherly already. . . .'

'Duke? A curious man, is he not?'

'Curious? I could come up with a hundred words that would fit him better.'

'Yes, I imagine you could,' Priest said, his smile thinning. 'But his character is unimportant to me.' Priest rose and parted the sheer curtains, looking out. With his back to Ray, the outlaw lord said, 'I can't have you bringing a herd of cattle through here, Mr Hardin – you should understand that.'

'I'm starting to.'

'No,' Priest said, letting the curtain fall closed. He turned to face Ray. 'That would cause me considerable, unwanted problems.' He returned to the table and seated himself again. Ashes fell from the cigar tip and landed on Blue Moon's pressed trousers. He brushed them away.

'Hardin, we have here a safe refuge for my men to return to after conducting their business. There are no hostile Indians in the vicinity, and the army does not know that we are up here. No one does – but you.'

'Me and Lyle Wycherly.'

Blue Moon made an indifferent shrug. 'Duke, weak and incapable as he is, would never report our presence to anyone. He knows that something unpleasant would be bound to follow.' The light went out of Priest's eyes briefly, and Ray could see the soul of a brutal outlaw chief behind them. Priest smiled again, and the expression vanished from his eyes.

'Are you telling me that something unpleasant can happen to me?' Ray said, shifting as much as he could in the chair. He had lost much circulation in both arms and legs. Priest laughed, and it was not the pleasant laugh of a merry man. He choked briefly on cigar smoke, coughed and wiped his eyes.

'There shouldn't be any question of that,' Blue Moon said, when he was able to speak again. 'To you and to your friends as well.'

'All right,' Ray said, weary of this conversation, of being bound, of the ache in his head and Blue Moon Priest all at once. 'What do you want?'

'What I *don't* want is a herd of cows being driven up here, my men having to battle a bunch of wild-eyed cowboys, someone running to the army for help. They would drive us out of the Poconos, and though our town might not seem to be much to you, it suits us as a base of operations, a place to recuperate for those who need that, a place to simply sleep where a posse or the army has no chance of stumbling upon a night camp.'

'I can understand that,' Ray said, locking eyes with the

bandit king. 'What I'm asking is what you want from me.'

'Simply put,' Priest said, rising to his feet, looking stern now though his smile was still in place. The sunlight caught his diamond stickpin and caused it to shine like cool fire. 'I want you to forget about this place. I want you to return and report that there is no suitable way through the Poconos for something as large as a herd of cattle. It will save me much trouble, and your people much blood.'

'And in return?' Ray ventured to ask.

'I will let you live,' Priest said in a low, calculated tone of voice. 'Allowing you to return is preferable – it will keep others from attempting to find a trail once you tell them that it is impossible. If you were to simply vanish, it would leave the question moot, and curiosity might spark another expedition. I want to put an end to speculation by having you report to your boss that it is an impossibility.'

'How do you know that's what I will say? Once I leave?'

'Hardin,' Priest asked, his eyes fixed steadily on Ray, 'do I have to keep the woman hostage? I don't want to, women are trouble, but if that's what it takes, I will do it. No one down below knows about her; no one will miss her or know she is gone.'

Ray shook his head violently, stirring his headache to life once more. 'No. You don't have to hold the woman. Will my word do it?' he asked.

'Your word is acceptable,' Priest said. 'Although I do have sources to inform me if you should break your pledge.'

'Sure; I wasn't forgetting Duke.'

'All right,' Priest said, not rubbing his hands together in satisfaction, but somehow giving the impression that that was what he was doing mentally. 'You will be shown a trail down to the east. Just make sure you do not head in the direction of Fort Davis when you leave here – there will be men watching you. If you were to do so, you would be tracked down and killed – the three of you.'

'I believe you,' Ray said sullenly.

'So long as we understand each other,' Priest said, now smiling, expansive again. 'You'll be given what supplies you need. Take your squaw and get off along the trail. If you ever come near here again, I'll have you shot dead on sight – do we understand each other?'

'Very well,' Ray said.

'Then!' Priest said, his cigar in his clenched teeth now. He withdrew a narrow, sharp knife from its sheath at the back of his belt and freed Ray's arms and feet with three swift, dangerous strokes of the blade. 'Get the hell out of my town and out of the Poconos. You know the southern route home well enough – use it.' He paused before exiting. 'Mister Hardin, count yourself lucky.'

SEVEN

Wally Chambers and Kata were waiting in front of the storehouse. Both looked relieved yet apprehensive as Ray limped toward them, his holster empty, his face battered, the shoulder of one shirtsleeve ripped open. 'Sonny', Ray's thick-chested jailer, was his escort as he stepped down off the dilapidated plankwalk and stumbled toward his friends, who waited with the two horses and Bess. The man wearing the faded blue cavalry shirt stood nearby, watching Kata and Wally.

Approaching them, Ray could see that they had had a rough time of it themselves. Wally's holster was also empty. There was a swollen bruise on the side of his face, and the knuckles of his hands were scraped and raw. A couple of fingers on his right hand looked as if they might be broken. Kata's face was grim. Her hair was tangled wildly and festooned with cobwebs. Her face was dirty, her mouth determined.

'Where'd they have you, Wally?' Ray asked.

'They jumped me, knocked down Kata, who tried to come to my assistance. After a brief scrap they hauled us off to some shed and threw us in. What about you, Ray? Where'd they take you?'

'To meet the boss,' Ray told him.

'Blue Moon? What sort of man does he seem to be?' Wally wanted to know.

'He's a volcano – you wouldn't want to be around him when he erupts.'

'No,' Wally agreed. 'What did he tell you?'

'He said to grab some supplies and get the hell out of his town.'

'That's all right with me. Anything else?'

'I'll tell you on the trail. Right now we'd better do what we were told.'

Kata had been watching their exchange fearfully, not having understood any of it. She followed them along to the storage building where Ray and Wally grabbed up as much as they could find as quickly as they could. This was not a casual shopping trip. Sacking what they could, which included anything edible for the long trail back, they loosely slung, but securely tied the load on Bess's back; they could not afford to lose these meager supplies.

Ray noticed that both of their rifle scabbards were empty. Well, why should he have expected anything else? He spoke in a low voice to Wally as they tightened the knots holding the mule's load.

'Did they get into my saddle-bags, Wally?'

'Not that I'm aware of. Why?'

'Because we may still have our four spare revolvers in there. And we might need them.'

Someone barked at them impatiently, 'OK, cowboys!

Let's get riding. I'm supposed to show you the trail out and I've got other things I'd prefer to be doing with my day.' The speaker was the outlaw in the cavalry shirt. Ray nodded, and with a quick check of his cinches he swung aboard his paint pony.

They lined out then, riding over barren land weaving through gigantic stacks of weather-cracked white boulders. The dust and the heat were oppressive in this chamber of stone where no breeze could reach them.

Twice the man with the white eyebrows waved up to watchers among the rocks, then proceeded on his way. The path they followed was confusing. It was meant to be. Once strangers were escorted from the outlaw camp, it was intended that finding their way back again would be impossible. Now and then Ray glimpsed a cut-off he thought would be wide enough for a herd of cattle to pass through, if driven that way.

He gave the matter little consideration. That part of the job was at an end. The Broken W would never drive a herd this way no matter what. He would report the Poconos impassable as he had been instructed by Blue Moon. If not because of his promise to the outlaw chief, to protect the Broken W hands who would not have a chance against the outlaw gang among these boulders. He would lie to his boss to save him from certain doom. He would not report Blue Moon's presence. He had given his word, for one thing, in order to free Wally and Kata.

For another, Jack Priest, if prodded, was perfectly capable of erupting, of sending his men swarming down on the Broken W where Glen Wycherly had tried to build a safe, secure home for his children.

Ray Hardin had no doubt that the small depredations would continue as Wycherly tried to drive the new herd to Fort Davis along the southern route past the foot of the Holden Range, but the alternative could be disastrous to the old man and his fortunes. Ray did wish that he could come up with a way to totally ruin Lyle Wycherly, who was apparently bent not only on destroying his father, but depleting his sisters' inheritance.

They did not speak of any of this until the man who was guiding them halted at the crest of a narrow, winding trail leading down to the white flats below.

'This is as far as I go, boys,' the man with the woolly white eyebrows said. 'You should know the road home. I guess Blue Moon must have told you what would happen if you try to come back.'

'I got the idea,' Ray Hardin said.

'Then, scat, damn you!'

They scatted. There was a heavy breeze now that they had emerged from the confused stack of boulders, and it drove against them as they angled their horses down the long slope, Kata following aboard patient Bess's back.

'Don't even look in the other direction,' Ray Hardin told Wally as they reached the flats.

'Toward Fort Davis? Why should I?'

'Just don't.'

Reaching level ground, they found the land familiar. Ray Hardin had been over the trail to Fort Davis three times, Wally twice before, pushing beeves. There was still a light breeze stirring, which was welcome. The trail stretched out straight and mostly smooth as they turned their horses westward toward the home ranch.

The country was mostly white with sage and greasewood everywhere, with now and then clumps of stunted juniper, manzanita and cholla cactus. Yellow buffalo grass had survived the winter frost here and there. The land was busy with spotted vegetation except along the wide swatch that herds of Broken W cattle had trampled into a broad white path over the years.

They rode along the empty trail; there was no sense in making things harder on themselves.

'All right,' Wally said, after they had ridden three or four miles down the road. 'What did Blue Moon say to you?'

'He said that he wouldn't tolerate anyone trying to drive cattle through his camp, that I was to tell Glen Wycherly that without mentioning the fact that there was an outlaw town up there.'

'What are you gong to do, Ray?'

'Just what Blue Moon suggested. I'll tell Wycherly that there's no safe trail through the Poconos.'

'You'd lie to the old man?' Wally asked, a little startled by Ray's decision.

'Not exactly. I'll just tell him there is no suitable trail through the Poconos. Which is the truth.' He glanced at Wally. 'Otherwise the Broken W will find itself in a battle it's not equipped to handle.'

'The army could be notified,' Wally replied.

'No, it can't,' Ray said firmly. 'Blue Moon as much as said he'd raze the Broken W, drive off the cattle and burn the houses. You think that would be helping Glen

Wycherly? He wouldn't survive such an attack.'

'Nor would the women, they'd be ruined.' Wally suddenly, inappropriately, grinned. 'Just when you've got Patricia fixed in your sights, and a nice house ready for you to move into – all just for taking a bath now and then.'

'Wally. . . .' Ray said. His patience was wearing thin on the topic.

'I know, Ray!' Wally said, laughing.

'I'll say it anyway – shut up!'

They plodded along in silence for a few more miles before Wally broached the subject that had been on his mind. 'What am I to do with Kata, Ray?'

'I guess that's something you'll just have to figure out,' Ray said. He was still a little miffed.

'I've been trying, but there's just nothing I can come up with.'

'What do you want to do with her?' Ray asked.

'That's not the point,' Wally said, his face looking drawn and suddenly weary. 'I mean, there's nothing I can do with her. I can't abandon her and I can't keep her with me. Not if I continue to work for Broken W. And what else can I do? I could hook up with another ranch, but the problem would be the same.'

Ray understood. There was no room in the bunkhouse for a woman. She could not just be sent off to camp out on her own. To Kata, Wally was her savior, a man who certainly had everything planned out. She could know nothing of cattle ranches and the way the hands lived.

'The woman would do anything for me, Ray! You

should have seen the way she fought for me back there. Tooth and nail when those men jumped me in the street.'

'Maybe the kindest thing to do would be to split the provisions and send her back into the hills. At least she knows the land, knows how to survive up there.' Even as Ray was speaking he could see Kata's adoring eyes on Wally. She was a lost animal, safe now. How could Wally simply chase her away, rejecting her friendship?

'Maybe something will occur to you,' Ray said unconvincingly. 'Let's pull up here for awhile.' He nodded toward a flat pond about an acre in size, its face a dull, leaden color. The animals had not been watered for awhile.

Wally, still lost in gloom, only nodded. There were shaggy willow trees standing near the pond, just beginning to bud into their spring greenery. They dismounted, slipped the bits from the horses and led them to water. Ray went to his paint's saddle-bags and sighed aloud with relief.

'They missed these, or didn't bother looking for them,' Ray said with satisfaction. He held a brace of new Colt .44 revolvers in his hands. There were two more in the opposite saddle-bag, and many boxes of ammunition. He handed one to Wally and opened the loading gate on the other, spinning the cylinder to assure himself that the pistol carried a full load of shells.

'That's better,' Wally said with a smile, settling the Colt into his holster. 'I was feeling a little naked.'

'What do you say we camp here?' Ray asked. 'I can't

recall another watering spot nearby, can you?'

'No, I can't remember one.' Although they only traveled the south road once a year in the spring, the trail was pretty much committed to memory. Water was all-important to a cattle drive. Had there been a place farther along that they could reach before sundown, they would have remembered it.

Wally glanced at the lowering sun. They had only a few hours of daylight remaining. 'It's probably best to call a halt. I'm getting pretty hungry anyway.'

'See what you can find to cook up,' Ray said. 'I know we didn't have time to do much shopping. Whatever will keep us alive is fine. I'll gather up some dead wood.'

'Ray,' Wally asked with some concern, 'you don't figure those men will be riding after us?' His eyes had shifted toward the east.

'What for?' Ray said. 'I don't see what reason there could possibly be for Blue Moon to set riders on our trail.'

'I don't either,' Wally admitted. 'I guess I'm getting nervous in my old age.'

Ray continued rummaging through his saddle-bags as the paint pony drank, unconcerned with the human's movements. The sun had lowered just enough so that the pond gleamed like silver in the slanting light. Shadows crept out from the willows. Kata, squatting by the pond, drank from her cupped hand, looking quite pretty and very young.

'They didn't take a thing,' Ray announced. 'Probably didn't bother. It's pretty obvious that we would have nothing they needed. Wally?'

Wally's head came up; he had been watching Kata crouched at the water's edge.

'What is it?'

'I've still got that block of lye soap.'

'Fine. Why are you telling me, Ray?'

'Here's soap,' Ray said in slow demonstration, 'there's water.'

'Well, aren't you . . . Miss Patricia has changed your whole personality, Ray.'

'Wally, I meant the woman might care to clean up again.' He tossed Wally the block of yellow soap. 'You can continue to stink if it suits you. I'm going to scrounge up some wood.'

'Stink?' Wally repeated in a low tone, followed by a few muttered, unintelligible words as Ray went on his way, smiling to himself.

It didn't take Ray long to gather an armload of dry, shaggy-barked willow branches from beneath the trees. When he returned he dropped the pile near a suitable campsite. Looking around as the sun slanted low and the western skies began to color in anticipation of nightfall, he searched with his eyes, but could not see Kata and Wally. Frowning he looked toward the pond, hearing a burst of laughter.

The two stood stripped in waist-deep water like innocents, splashing each other with water. Ray shook his head, rubbed the rough bark from the willow branches for tinder and started a fire. Wally returned a quarter of an hour on, his wet blond hair slicked back, buttoning his shirt.

'You know, Ray, once you get used to it, those baths aren't a bad idea.'

Ray fought to hold back a grin. He watched as Wally fed the fire to get it to his liking, filled a pan with sliced bacon and started it frying. Kata approached them from the pond, her long dark hair still damp, looking like a water nymph in the rosy glow of sunset. She went immediately toward Wally and squatted down beside him in the light of the fire. The two smiled those secret sorts of smiles you saw on young lovers' faces.

Yes, indeed, Ray thought, Wally Chambers was going to have a tough time giving the Indian woman up.

Ray went to his saddle-bags, now placed beneath a scraggly tree beside his saddle and bedroll, and unbuckled them again. After giving the matter some thought, he took one of the two remaining Colts from the bags and walked to the fire where Wally had pan-bread started.

'Kata,' Ray said, startling the girl. Ray realized he had seldom, if ever, spoken directly to Kata, and that was what had alarmed her. Her eyes were almost fearful when she looked up at Wall-ee's tall chief, wondering if she had done something wrong.

'Here, you'd better take this,' Ray Hardin said, handing her the spanking new Colt revolver. 'You might need it.'

Kata cradled the weapon in her hands, her expression brightening. The tall chief had given her a sign that she had been accepted into the tribe. Her lips quivered, pursed, and then she said quite distinctly, 'Thank you.'

Wally laughed with pride. 'Isn't she something, Ray? I've determined to teach her a word or two every day. It won't take her long to learn – she's smart as a whip.'

Ray looked at both of them. His happiness for them was real but tempered by the realization that there was a different world at trail's end, a world where Kata did not belong. Well, let them have their few days of contentment.

'Make sure she knows how to handle that pistol, Wally,' was all he said.

They made their beds and turned in early. They still had three days' travel ahead of them before they reached the Broken W again. *Broken,* was it not? Ray Hardin considered just before he fell off to sleep. Glen Wycherly trying to hold on to the end while his son, Lyle, was trying to steal the ranch away from him; while Louise glided about in her fancy clothes, unconcerned about the ranch but only the income it could produce; while poor, faithful, lost Patricia Wycherly scurried about working as hard as any servant; while the wild, careless Josie Wycherly stormed about the ranch causing trouble wherever she went.

Ray Hardin had always wished he had his own ranch. At times he thought of having children. If that was where all dreams led. . . .

He was asleep before he could finish his gloomy thought.

They came in the hour before dawn. Ray heard the close explosion of a gun being touched off. At the same time sand rose from beside his bed and spattered his face. He rolled to one side, slapping for his own weapon as three more shots were fired – two from the willow trees and one from their own camp. Ray managed to reach his horse on hands and knees. The paint was excited, disturbed in its sleep as it had been, but stood still except for the quivering beneath its patchy hide. As a temporary bulwark, the horse's body was fine, but Ray could not risk the horse being shot, leaving him stranded afoot in this country, and he regretted taking shelter behind it for that reason.

Looking past the pony's neck, he saw the not-so-stealthy shadow of a man rushing through the willows. Ray loosed a shot, but in that light, under those conditions, he missed, the bullet spanging off the trunk of a shaggy willow.

From somewhere in the willows another gun fired twice, neither shot aimed at Ray. From their own camp someone fired back, three rapidly exploding shots, and an attacker in the woods let out a howl of pain. Ray held his position, thumb wrapped round the hammer of his Colt, his other hand stroking the neck of the paint, wanting to keep it steady. If it ran, it would be disastrous. One brown, pleading eye rolled back to look at Ray. 'What are you doing?' the horse seemed to want to know.

Ray stayed where he was. There was little point in moving, He could not rush the woods on foot, could not mount his horse and charge, could not dive toward another sheltered place: there was none.

There was a rustling in the willows and then the sounds

of horses being ridden away hastily in the night. When the sound of retreating hoofs was no longer audible, Ray slipped away from behind the horse and went to where Kata and Wally had been sleeping. Ray was all right, but what about the others?

He found Wally Chambers on his knees, dressed in his long johns, pale hair in his eyes, his revolver in hand. Kata sat beside him, her new pistol on her lap.

'Are you all right?' Ray asked.

'Not a scratch,' Wally panted, 'but it was a near thing.' He held up his blanket, which had a still-smoldering hole in it.

'It's a good thing one of us was awake,' Ray said, examining the blanket by the feeble glow of the waning moon.

'One of us – but it wasn't me,' Wally said, bowing his head in Kata's direction.

'Shoot, shoot,' Kata said; that must have been her new word for the day. She held up the Colt revolver that Ray had given her.

'Yes, and she plugged one of them,' Wally said proudly. 'I wasn't wearing my belt gun when those coyotes slunk in here. To shoot a man in his bed! Ray, I thought you told us that Blue Moon was not going to be sending any of his men after us.'

'I don't think it was any of Jack Priest's outlaws,' Ray said, standing, looking out at the night.

'Who then? Highwaymen?'

'Your friend Duke,' Ray believed.

'Lyle Wycherly?' Wally was incredulous. 'Why? We're his own men, and we're headed back to the ranch.'

'Yes,' Ray agreed, 'but he still doesn't know what we intend to tell his father. He can't let Glen learn that he is practically an ally of the outlaw gang, that he's been tipping them off for years about when the herds would be driven though to Fort Davis.'

'I'll be damned,' Wally muttered. 'Then that would probably have been Sully Parks and Brian Akers with him. They would gun down their own saddle partners as they slept? Why, Ray?'

'They're all in this together now, Wally, and they're desperate men.'

'But you're not even going to say anything to Glen Wycherly about the outlaws or his son!'

'They don't know that. They have a lot to lose, especially Lyle. His position, his inheritance. . . .' Ray paused; he was about to say 'and his father's love', but he didn't think that something so trivial as that would mean anything to a man like Lyle Wycherly.

'Shoot,' Kata said again, holding out her weapon.

'Yes, Kata,' Wally said, putting his arm around her shoulders, smiling at her. 'And to think that I owe my life to a woman I've only just met, and men I've worked with for years tried to gun me down in my bed!'

'Life is a cruel sport,' Ray said. Wally figured he was quoting somebody, but he only nodded his head.

'She hit one of them,' Wally said, stepping into his jeans as they spoke. 'Any idea which one?'

Ray, who had had only a fleeting glimpse of the men, answered, 'The big man. If it was those three it had to be Sully Parks. We'll find out when we get back to the Broken W. It's pretty hard to hide a bullet hole.'

'If we get back,' Wally said, buttoning his shirt. In the east the sky was beginning to gray along the line of the horizon. Dawn was not far off. 'We've still got what? Three days in open country?'

'We'll just have to keep a closer eye on our surroundings. It's pretty hard to slip on a man unseen out here unless you're an Apache.'

'Apache!' Kata was suddenly animated. She got to her feet in one fluid motion and exclaimed, 'Shoot, shoot!'

Wally Chambers smiled and told Ray, 'I'll throw something together for breakfast.'

Despite their fears, they saw no more of the raiders as they traveled their way back to the Broken W. It was warm along the trail, but not that warm; cool at night, but not too cool. From springs far up in the Holden Range water seeped and trickled out onto the flats. Bright new grass was beginning to sprout everywhere. They saw hundreds of young cottontail rabbits feeding on the green grass, and here and there a deer browsed. All of the familiar ponds they passed were filled with water.

'Give the grass another week or so and the time for a drive will be right,' Wally commented.

'That's what I plan to report to Glen Wycherly, although the man has been on the land for thirty years, and doesn't need me to tell him that.'

'And the other. . . ?' Wally asked.

Ray shook his head. 'Nothing about outlaws, nothing about his son. Why add to his woes?'

'Besides, you gave your word to Blue Moon.'

'Besides, I gave my word.' And a man does not break his word. Not in the West, at least. They had no lawyers, no contracts, few laws. A man's word counted for all if it was good. If his word was not, no business would be done with him. Any trust in him was destroyed if his word was broken once given.

'Oh, well!' Wally said rather loudly. It was frustration. It seemed that they had been through a lot for nothing.

'It is a bad day,' Kata said from Bess's back, where she rode beside Wally. She waited for his approval, and he grinned at her.

'You're doing good, Kata,' Ray told her. 'Wally is a fine teacher.'

'Wall-ee is a good man,' Kata said, proud of herself.

Wally Chambers's face had fallen. Ray knew what he was thinking as they neared the end of the long trail. What was to be done with the Indian girl? She was such a faithful dog to Wally. Ray had made the mistake of using that term in front of Wally one day and the blond kid erupted.

'I won't let her be seen that way. She's faithful, loyal – she would die for me, but she's a fine woman, not a dog.'

'It was an unhappy choice of words,' Ray said, trying to apologize, but Wally simmered over that remark for most of the day.

Now, not far ahead they could see smoke rising in a thin, straight line to meet the sky. They could make out groves of live-oak trees, and here and there were a few stray cows which they only briefly considered hieing back toward the ranch.

They had come home to the Broken W. What the ranch held for each of them was impossible to guess.

EIGHT

'Well, I guess I'd better head up to the big house first off,' Ray said, as they approached the white ranch houses through the trees.

'Are you sure that you don't want to brush your teeth and take a bath first?' Wally gibed. You know Patricia will be waiting.'

'Are you ever going to outgrow that tired joke?' Ray asked peevishly. The rising breeze through the oaks was fresh and swift. Ray watched the skies for awhile. Wally finally nudged him.

'You can't put it off, Ray.'

'I know. I just wish that I could tell Mr Wycherly everything that we found out.'

'Maybe he's better off not knowing,' Wally said.

Ray took a deep, slow breath and answered. 'You may be right,' he said, swinging down from his paint horse. 'What man would want to be told that his son was plotting against him? I'll just tell him what we've decided on. What are you going to do, Wally?' he asked, glancing at Kata, who still sat the mule, expecting nothing but showing confidence in the ability of these two men to handle matters. Such unwarranted faith in them was a little unnerving.

'We'll just wait here for awhile, Ray. Tell us all about it when you come back – I've some decisions to make.'

Ray lumbered toward the house, leading the paint, which he hitched loosely in front of the wide porch of the big house. Dusting off as best he could, he stepped up onto the porch and rapped on the door. Patricia opened the door wearing a white cotton dress with small blue flowers embroidered on it. She looked surprised to see him, almost shocked. She had little to say, but then she never did.

'Father's in his office,' Patricia said, gesturing. Ray knew the way and so he started on across the hardwood floor of the big living room. Glancing up he saw the figure of Louise Wycherly at the top of the stairs. She was dressed in black as usual, watching him without pleasure. She had never approved of simple cowhands coming into the house. Ray nodded to her in passing and she turned away sharply as if he had hurled an insult at her.

Glen Wycherly was at his desk, his elbows on the surface, his face held in his cupped hands. There was a glass of whiskey beside his elbow although the hour was early. The old man did not look well. The tan on his wrinkled face was fading; his white hair was unbrushed. When he looked up to find Ray in the room, his pale-blue eyes were clouded. Wycherly managed a small, genuine smile, and he rose shakily to take Ray's hand.

'Take a seat, please, Ray. I was starting to wonder if

you would make it back. I was starting to feel guilty about even having sent you into the Poconos. Sit down and tell me – how did it go up there?'

'Not well, sir. There's no way a herd of steers could be driven that way.'

'Well, I'd hoped so, but not really expected it, Ray. I told you before you left, there is no shame attached to failing a job that could not have been accomplished. It was only the desperate whim of an old man. We lose enough cattle every year on the southern trail that it cuts my operating margin to the bone.'

'The grass is looking good along the trail,' Ray told him, 'and there's plenty of water.'

'You returned that way?'

'Yes, we found a trail – not much more than a donkey track – down the eastern slope of the Poconos and decided to return via the southern route, since it is familiar to both of us.'

'Ray,' Glen said, leaning back in his chair. He hesitated, his hand stretched out for the empty whiskey glass and fell away again. 'I want you to ramrod the trail drive this year.'

'But Lyle will—'

'I haven't seen Lyle for more than a week,' Wycherly said tautly. 'He didn't tell me he was leaving or why.'

'Oh,' was all Ray could think of to say under the circumstances.

'Take a day or two to rest up,' Wycherly told him. 'I'll have Travis Knight continue overseeing the gather. He's a good hand.'

'Yes,' Ray agreed, 'he is.'

'You've been over that southern trail with a herd a couple of times—'

'Three times on trail drives.'

'Yes, well then, you pretty much know my policies. If the Indians try to threaten you, let them have a few beeves to satisfy them. We don't need a war out there. If it's a small-time rustler, a sodbuster who might need food for his family, turn a blind eye unless it gets out of hand. If you get hit by one of the big bands of outlaws, you'll probably have to fight. They'll try to drive off a hundred steers in one fell swoop, and I can't afford to lose that many beeves – not just now.'

'We'll protect the herd,' Ray answered.

'I know you will try, Ray. I just hate the idea of losing a single hand guarding my steers.' His regretful expression was genuine. Glen Wycherly rose, seeming to have to pry himself up out of his chair, and walked stiffly to where his whiskey was kept. 'Are you all right, Ray – physically, I mean?'

Ray realized his face had not yet healed from the beating he had taken. 'Just a few scrapes and bruises,' Ray told the ranch owner. 'I'm fine.'

'Stay around the ranch tomorrow at least. I want you in top shape for the drive.'

'All right. I'd like Wally Chambers as my *segundo*, if that's all right with you.'

'You're trail boss, that's up to you. How is Chambers?' Glen Wycherly asked, sipping at a fresh glass.

'He's fine, it's just that he has a small problem he's unable to solve just now.'

'Oh?' Wycherly's white eyebrows arched. 'Anything I can do to help? What is this problem, exactly?'

Ray hesitated – how to explain it? 'He's brought a woman back to the ranch.'

'A woman?' Wycherly's face grew briefly puzzled. He sipped again at his drink.

'An Indian girl. He sort of found her up in the Poconos.'

'Not an Apache woman!' Wycherly asked. He had spent a large part of his youth fighting Apaches as he built the Broken W.

'No, sir. We think she's a Jumano girl.'

'Jumano? I didn't think there were any left around.'

'There aren't, except for this one woman,' Ray said carefully. 'Wally has gotten quite attached to her. He's considering quitting the job and going somewhere where he can find a way to take care of her.'

'That serious, is it?' Glen said, tilting back in his chair, hands folded together over his stomach. 'Well, we can't lose a good man like Chambers this time of year.' He was briefly thoughtful. 'Can the woman cook?'

'I don't think so. Not what we'd consider cooking.'

'How about washing up? Cleaning the house?'

'She could do that, she would, willingly,' Ray said without having consulted Wally or Kata.

'Well, then,' Wycherly said, 'there's no real problem. She can stay on for at least a week or so while you and Chambers are on your trail drive. We've several servants' rooms in the back of the house. Empty. Help is hard to find out here, as you can imagine. If she works out she can stay indefinitely.'

'I'll tell Wally,' Ray said, rising from his chair. 'It'll relieve his mind, at least for a while.'

Ray planted his hat on his head and smiled. 'Her name is Kata – she only speaks a few words of English now, but Wally has been trying to teach her more.'

Wycherly was on his feet again. He threw an arm over Ray's shoulders.

'We'll take care of Kata, Ray. Chambers doesn't have to worry about her.'

'You want me to talk to Travis Knight, or will you?' Ray asked.

'I'll call him in. There's a few places I want to remind him where the steers like to hide out.'

Ray wanted to say more, could not. Surprisingly, as they walked toward the office door, Wycherly said, 'Ray, I know something about my son's activities, more than Lyle thinks I do.'

Ray Hardin was stuck for a response. Wycherly went on, 'What the young fool doesn't realize is that, intent on immediate rewards, he will lose any of his rights to the Broken W. I don't mean that to be vindictive, but I can't have such a man running this ranch. It pains me to do it, but he's been cut out of my will. My daughter is a better choice to manage the Broken W.'

'Yes,' Ray replied, as they stood halted in the open doorway. 'I can see that Patricia would be—'

He got no further with his sentence. Glen Wycherly had broken into a deep, dry laugh which seemed ready to double him up at the waist. He took hold of Ray's arm at the elbow, straightened himself and wiped a tear from the corner of his eye.

'Don't you see, Ray – no, how could you know? They were in it together, a game called tricking the old man. I've had the books Patricia kept examined. Thousands of dollars have been skimmed off over the past few years. They're driving the Broken W into the ground. Louise was complicit in all of this. She may have been the one to first convince the others to join the game. She does like to have money to trifle away on her extravagances.

'No, Ray my friend, when I am gone the ranch will fall into the possession of Josie.'

Josie?

The wild little red-haired tomboy? She was to become the heir of the Broken W?

'Ray,' Wycherly was saying, 'I told you that I was aware of a lot of things going on around me that others thought I knew nothing about. Now, I have to tell you one thing that is for your own good, Ray: you do not know Josie. Not a thing about her.'

Glen Wycherly ended with a wink at Ray and returned to his desk and his whiskey, leaving Ray with a puzzling welter of emotion and thoughts. As he crossed the living room again, he considered that at least he did have some good news for Wally and Kata, if both of them agreed to Wycherly's offer of a job. Why not, at least on a temporary basis? That would free Wally of his worries at least long enough to help him organize the trail drive and provide temporary accommodation for Kata. It seemed a fair idea to Ray Hardin, but then he was not Wally Chambers, and certainly not Kata. What they would think of the offer was another matter.

He found them standing in the cool shade of the oak trees. Wally looked worried, Kata, who could not know what was going on, wearing a puzzled expression.

'Well?' Wally asked, looking up at the taller man.

'The old man says that Kata can stay on, live in the servants' quarters in the big house – if she's willing. I asked for you as *segundo* to side me on the drive to Fort Davis. We'll be gone a week, ten days. I don't know how you can explain any of this to her. But it is a temporary solution to your problems.'

'Temporary, yes. I'll come back to the same situation, won't I? As for Kata staying in the house, working for the Wycherlys, I don't know how she'd like that.' Wally frowned. 'Being held inside . . . you know, Ray, that locking an Indian in jail for a month is the same as life imprisonment to them. They are born free, raised free. Four walls are like cages to them.'

'The big house is hardly a jail,' Ray objected.

'Not to us, no. Kata might feel differently about matters. Especially if I can't find some way to assure her that I'm coming back soon.'

'I can't help you with that,' Ray said. 'You'll have to do some thinking on it.'

As he was speaking a whirlwind arrived from the north. A wild, redheaded whirlwind with a pack of dogs panting after her red roan, too exhausted to yap. She spotted the trio standing in the trees and turned her weary horse's head that way.

'What's she want?' Wally asked sourly.

'Careful what you say in front of your future boss,' Ray Hardin said, and Wally gave him an astonished look.

'I'll tell you later, Wally.'

Josie Wycherly seemed to lightly bounce out of the saddle and hit the ground as softly as a cat. She was wearing jeans, half-boots and a suede leather jacket over a long-sleeved white blouse. Her legs were long for her height, Ray noticed. Her small body was healthy, trim, as it would be for any woman who rode as much as she did. Her red hair was wind-twisted, but her face was not flushed, nor did she seem short of breath as she strode up to them, tapping her riding quirt against her leg.

'What kind of game are you three playing, hiding out here in the trees?' Only one of the dogs had followed her, a big black beast with yellow eyes and fearsome fangs. The rest had run to water or collapsed on their bellies, watching, pink tongues panting. The black dog sniffed at Kata, and growled. Ranch dogs are trained to know an Indian's scent. It alerts them to lurking raiders. The dog knew that this stranger did not smell of sugar, salt, tobacco or alcohol. Josie tapped the big dog on the nose with her quirt.

'Go home, Bear!' she commanded, although the dog was home. It slunk away, turning its head back twice to show a menacing set of bared fangs. 'Who's this, then?' she asked, studying Kata.

Ray spoke for them. 'Her name is Kata, and she's a friend of Wally's.'

'That so?' she asked, studying Kata more closely. 'Looks like you've been long on the trail.'

'Through the Poconos and back,' Ray told her. 'Your father has told us that Kata can stay in the servants' quarters and work in the kitchen.'

Josie laughed. 'No! My father means well, but he is getting older.'

'You mean. . . ?' Wally began weakly.

'I mean,' the redhead said, 'we have a perfectly good guest house going unused on this ranch, and if she is a friend of yours, Chambers, she is a guest here.' She added after a moment, 'And we do not put our guests to work.'

'Miss Josie. . . .' Again Wally couldn't finish his sentence.

'I'm taking charge here if no one objects.' She smiled at Kata. 'We'll be happy to give you a comfortable room, and after the trail, you'll want a hot bath first thing. I'll set some of the boys to heating some water. If you'll come with me.' She beckoned and after a hesitant glance at Wally, who nodded, Kata followed Josie toward the white guest house.

Wally, hands on hips, stood watching in amazement as the two women walked away, Josie leading her horse, holding Kata's with her free hand. She was speaking animatedly to the Jumano woman, who could not have understood a word of whatever Josie was saying. They disappeared into the small house.

Wally, seeming stunned, turned toward Ray Hardin. 'If that woman is going to be our new boss one day, I can live with that.'

They led their tired horses and Bess away toward the stable. Wally was still shaking his head. 'A hot bath,' he said in wonder. 'Probably be giving her a toothbrush next. Those notions must run in the family.'

'Taking Kata in like that was a kind gesture,' Ray

observed. 'I doubt either of her sisters would have done that. I guess old Glen Wycherly was right: I don't know Josie, not a thing about her.'

'Well, she just showed us something about herself,' Wally said.

'It'll keep Kata more comfortable. Josie can teach her a few more words. Maybe the two will even become friends.'

'Do you think so, Ray? I guess it's possible. I know it will make my time away from Kata a little easier, knowing she's being taken care of.'

'Sure it will. I've got to unsaddle and find Travis Knight. Wycherly wants to see him.'

'All right,' Wally said. 'I'll be happy just to get back to the bunkhouse, eat someone else's cooking and hit my bed early.'

'Don't forget that Brian Akers and Sully Parker might be around somewhere and that could mean trouble.'

'I haven't forgotten about those two snakes. If I do run into Sully I might ask him to show me where the girl shot him.'

Ray smiled despite the fact that their situation was still dangerous. This was one year he'd be happy to have the round-up finished and start the cows forward on the long trail drive to Fort Davis. They should be ready to start in two or three days. He would ask Travis Knight how the gather was coming along. Leaving that many cattle milling in one place for too long could lead to discontent and even clashes among the steers. It was best to get them moving as soon as the hands had taken a day's rest or so and the chuck wagon had been stocked with provisions.

At the open double doors to the stable they came face to face with Lyle Wycherly. The young man, dressed now in white buckskin trousers and a flaming red shirt with a blue scarf around his neck, seemed astonished to see them.

'You!' Lyle said in surprise. Then, 'I suppose you've been telling stories to my father.'

'No, there's no need to. I think your father has a pretty good idea of what's been going on around here.'

'That old fool?' Lyle scoffed. 'Not unless you've been filling his ear with your tales.'

'There are old fools around,' Ray said evenly. 'There are also a lot of clever, older men who know more than you could ever imagine. There's a whole lot more young fools who strut around believing they know everything.'

'Are you calling me. . . ?' Lyle's face infused with blood. His anger was apparent. 'Are you calling me. . . ?'

'No,' Ray said in a soothing voice. 'I didn't say that you were young, Lyle. You're getting a little long in the tooth to be considered young.' Ray shouldered past Lyle Wycherly and led his paint horse into the barn with Wally following. He couldn't resist one last shot at Wycherly, who still stood in the doorway, fuming.

'Here's one less thing for you to worry about: you won't be needed on the spring trail drive this year. Your father wants me to ramrod it.'

'Why, you. . . .' Lyle Wycherly let loose a string of

profanities which at least tied and maybe eclipsed all of his previous efforts.

'He'll kill you if he can,' Wally warned.

'He's already had his chance.'

'Yes, but, oh never mind, Ray. I just don't see the point in aggravating the man.'

'There's none really, but I enjoy trying to take him down a peg every chance I get. The man's a skunk.'

'Yes, he is,' Wally was forced to agree. 'But it's not a good idea to prod skunks too much.'

Ray had lifted his saddle from the paint's back and led it to a stall where it would have its first taste of oats in many a day. He began currying the horse as it nibbled at the food in the bin. Wally hadn't moved to work on his own horse yet. He was staring at the doorway.

'Watching for Lyle?' Ray gibed. He knew what was on Wally's mind: Kata's welfare was important to him. Wally tipped back his hat so that some of his thin blond hair spilled across his forehead.

'No, I was forgetting something,' Wally answered. 'Don't you think I'd better take Bess over to the big house before we get her bedded down? It could be they could use some of the provisions we've got left over from the trail.'

'That's a good idea,' Ray said, bending behind his pony to hide his grin. 'I hadn't thought of that.'

Wally stepped toward the door as a small stampede rushed across the yard. Josie off on another wild ride, the dogs in full pursuit. And just behind Josie Wycherly came another rider. Kata, who was unused to a saddle, was doing a good job of keeping up with Josie, hand-flagging the wild-eyed little sorrel she was riding. Josie let out a whoop and Kata followed with her own. The dogs broke into a frantic chorus of barking.

Wally watched them go by in a blur of color and motion. While the dust was still settling he turned back toward Ray and asked plaintively, 'What have we gone and done, Ray?'

NINE

Ray met Travis Knight on his way to the bunkhouse. The older foreman of the Broken W was sitting his bay horse and he walked the animal beside Ray Hardin as they talked.

'You already spoke with Glen Wycherly? That meeting didn't take long,' Ray commented.

'He just wanted to remind me about a few of the breaks where the strays like to hide. He does that every year. It's more of a ritual than anything else. I think he just wanted to inform me that you'd be honcho on this drive so there'd be no doubt about it.'

'Any objections?' Ray asked, cocking an eyebrow.

Travis Knight laughed. 'Makes me no difference. I get paid the same either way.'

'How's the round-up going?' Ray asked.

'We've just about gathered all we're going to find. Five hundred and fifty, I counted. That's a lot of beef, Ray.' He added, 'I'd say by the day after tomorrow we'll be ready to get them started. Do you want me to take care of seeing to the provisioning of the chuck wagon and warning Cooky that we're nearly ready to start the herd?'

'If you would. You've had the experience at organizing drives; I'm the new hand as far as that goes.'

'All right. I'll see that the wagon is fitted out, axles greased and ready to roll. Then I'll tell Cooky that he's got two days to get provisions loaded and his recipes in order.'

'You mean he actually uses recipes!' Ray asked.

'Just a little joke, boss. I'll see you this evening. We can talk things over in the bunkhouse.'

'Fine. Oh, Travis, don't count on Brian Akers or Sully Parks. They won't be going with us.'

Travis Knight frowned, shrugged and answered, 'I'll have to draft a couple of the stay-at-home hands to take their places. There's not a lot of cowboys wandering around loose way out here.'

'No, I know. Do your best, Travis.'

Travis Knight might have had a question or two for Ray, but he just swallowed them for the time being, nodded and went on his way.

Entering the bunkhouse, Ray found Lenny Polk sitting on his bed, worrying a loose nail in his boot with a hammer. A new-hire named Jason Wright was hovering near the iron stove, tin cup of coffee in his hand. Farther along the aisle Brian Akers and Sully Parker sat facing each other on adjacent bunks. Sully was facing the doorway and his wide face jerked up. The big man seemed to tremble a little and then he regained his habitual scowl.

'What are you two doing here?' Ray said, loudly enough for everyone to turn, paying attention. 'Don't you realize yet that you're finished on the Broken W?'

'Says who?' Sully asked truculently.

'You're as good as done. Go whining to Lyle Wycherly if you like. He's got nothing to do with things around here any longer.' Turning briefly toward the astonished Lenny Polk and Wright, Ray Hardin told them, 'Day after tomorrow we're starting the trail drive. Get back out and see if Knight needs any help organizing things.'

'Who do you think you are?' Brian Akers asked, coming to his feet.

'I'm ramrod for the trail drive. Duke is not going along. Neither are you two.'

'If I was able. . . .' Sully Parker growled, beginning a threat. The big man tried to rise from his bunk, but couldn't make it to his feet.

Ray asked, 'What's the matter, Sully? Have you showed the others where the girl shot you?'

'We were jumped by a band of rustlers,' Brian Akers said, his eyes going to Wright and Lenny Polk, asking for belief.

'Were you?' Ray asked. 'Was that before or after you tried to murder Wally Chambers and me in our beds and the girl shot Sully? Where's the bullet, Sully? In your leg?'

'I told you,' Akers repeated, determined to brazen it out, 'we were jumped—'

'You're forgetting, Brian, I was there!' Ray calmed

himself, for he found that his breathing was tight and his hands had clenched into fists out of anger. 'You better decide if you want to get off the Broken W now or wait until you're fired off it. Glen Wycherly knows all about it.'

'Duke will—'

'Duke won't do anything about it. Didn't I just tell you that Wycherly knows everything about what you three have been up to?'

'You told him?' Akers said. 'After. . . .' He had been about to invoke the name of Blue Moon Priest, but managed to stop himself from the virtual admission.

'Ah, you're just angry, Ray,' Sully Parker said with a smile that didn't fit well on his brutal face.

'You think I'm angry? Wait until Wally Chambers gets over here. Wally doesn't spend as much time talking things over as I do.'

They knew that to be true. With an air of resignation Akers reached under his bunk for his bedroll and nodded to Sully Parker. 'I guess we're done here, Sully.'

'I'm not quite done,' Sully Parker growled. 'Hardin, when I'm able I'm going to find you and shoot you to dog meat.'

Ray smiled. 'I'm a little better with a Colt than the Indian girl. When you're ready to make your try, I'll give you the chance. Assuming I'm not in bed sleeping.'

With that, Ray, his position established, threats made and promises extended, turned on his heel and went out with amazed stares from the young Lenny Polk and Jason Wright following him.

The sun was lowering toward the far horizon. The few scattered high clouds were beginning to take on a pinkish tint. Ray could see sifting dust settling above the oaks in front of the big house, indicating that Josie and Kata had returned from their short, wild ride early. He came upon Wally Chambers, trudging wearily toward the stable, leading his dun horse and old Bess. Ray took the mule's lead from Wally's gloved hands. The mule was unburdened.

'I guess Cooky wanted those supplies.'

'Not so much, I would guess, but he said there could never be too much food in storage around here. I helped him take the bags into the larder.' Wally was wearing an odd expression, a sort of happy frown.

Ray prompted him. 'What happened, Wally?'

'Well,' Wally said, halting his horse, 'Cooky and me were about done with our work when a lot of shrieking and yelling started up. Cooky beckoned me out onto the porch and we stood there, Cooky smoking his pipe, until the storm blew over.'

'Who was it?' Ray had to ask.

'Who it was, was Louise Wycherly. She was yelling at her father. The old man tried to turn a deaf ear and walk away, but she followed him out into the kitchen, keeping it up.'

'And you heard it all?'

'Couldn't help but. We were standing out on the porch, not ten feet away.'

'And?'

'First thing I could hear clearly was Miss Louise shouting, "She's not staying here, not in my house."

Meaning Kata. The old man, calm as you please, told her that she knew what the little house was for, visiting family and guests. And that he would eventually deed it over to whichever of his children got married first.

'Funny, Ray, the old man asked Louise if she had slipped out and gotten married in the past few days without telling him; if not, the little house was still for guests to use and Kata was Josie's guest and she had every right to be there.

'There was a lot more about the girl being a savage and Josie little better. And that they would probably destroy the house before they were finished.'

Wally started on leading his dun horse; Ray followed with Bess's lead in his hand.

'Before Louise was finished she shouted that Josie had always been the favorite because she was the youngest, Glen's little baby girl. Then she said something about Glen Wycherly getting old, his mind deteriorating . . . I didn't hear any more because Glen turned and walked away.' Wally laughed. 'Probably returning to his office for a stiff drink or two, which he deserved.'

As they entered the barn, Bess and the dun horse both livened up, scenting fresh hay and oats and anticipating a restful night in the stable after the deprivations of the long trail. Wally was finally able to shuck his saddle from the weary dun horse's back. Bess was freed of her gear, rubbed down some and led into a stall.

A thought had occurred to Ray, and he asked Wally

over a partition, 'Was Miss Patricia present when this all happened?'

'Almost. I caught a glimpse of her standing back in the hallway, arms crossed. She never said a word; you know how Patricia is.'

Did he? Ray Hardin wondered after his last conversation with Glen Wycherly. It would be easy to guess that while Louise blustered and screamed at her father, claiming her birthright, and Lyle plotted and stole from his father, Patricia, in a patient way which was her nature, only waited for matters to play out as they would. She virtually managed the finances of the ranch now and found herself uniquely indispensable to each and every one of them.

Patricia had time and she knew it, so long as she kept her head down and continued to play the shy, obedient daughter. That was pure speculation on Ray's part, of course. It could be that the retiring soul only wished to avoid confrontation and go on living as she always had, in her father's well-managed home.

'Anyway, that should mean that you haven't got to worry about Kata's welfare while we're gone – not if Glen Wycherly is on her side.'

'No,' Wally agreed glumly. 'All I have to worry about is her becoming like Josie, wilder than any wild Indian.'

'People don't suddenly go against their natures, Wally. Kata just needed to let off some steam and it was Josie's way of welcoming her as a friend.'

Wally had put his horse away. He stood dusting his hands together. His eyes fixed on Ray Hardin. 'It seems you're softening a bit toward Josie,' he said.

'I don't know what you mean,' Ray answered. 'Besides, I never had a thing against the girl in the first place.'

'Uh-huh,' Wally said to himself. Then, 'All right, Ray, what do we do now?'

'We get some sleep. Tomorrow we do nothing – give ourselves and our ponies some rest while Travis Knight gets the trail herd organized. I might not have had the chance to tell you, but you're my *segundo* on the drive.'

'You've kind of taken the reins out of Duke's hands, Ray – he won't like this a bit.'

'No, he won't,' Ray agreed, as they walked out of the stable into the purple twilight, 'but that's the way Glen Wycherly wanted it, and he's the boss, not his son.'

'Where do you think Duke is now?' Wally asked, as they scuffed their way toward the bunkhouse.

'If he has any sense, he's sitting down to supper with his family. If he doesn't, he's riding like fury to tell Blue Moon that our drive starts the day after tomorrow, and to get ready to raid the herd.'

'What do you think Priest will tell him?'

'Depends on how much he needs the cash right now, I expect. Cattle-rustling is not his preferred way of making a living.'

'Lamps are lit all through the bunkhouse, and I can smell steak frying, Ray. It's good to be back home.'

'When I was there last, Sully Parker was in the mood to fight,' Ray told his friend. 'Try to avoid a showdown if possible.'

'After the snake tried to kill me in my bed? They

might have killed Kata, too, you realize.'

'Just *try*,' Ray said, knowing how easily Wally Chambers could be triggered. 'I tried to run him and Brian Akers off the ranch, but I don't know if they left. We really don't need a shooting now when we're trying to get the herd to Fort Davis. The old man needs that money, not more trouble in the Broken W.'

Wally nodded as they approached the bunkhouse porch. He looked at his taller, darker friend and said, 'You know, Ray, I can remember a time when you would have—'

'I'm older now,' Ray told him. 'And a little calmer.'

'Older and ready to settle down?'

'What's that mean?' Ray asked. Wally was wearing that smirk of his again. It seemed that there was nothing that gave Wally Chambers more pleasure than ribbing Ray when the subject was women.

'Nothing, Ray!' Wally said, holding up both hands to protest his innocence.

Ray knew that Wally was now referring to Josie Wycherly. Ray regretted ever having said simply that he had nothing against the girl. Wally had built upon it as he had magnified the meaning of Patricia performing the simple gesture of giving Ray a toothbrush and a bar of soap.

'You can be wearying,' Ray said as they entered the bunkhouse, which was filled with the scents of tobacco and fried steaks, the sight of a dozen Broken W cowboys scattered about, some eating at the table, some relaxing on their bunks, rubbing tired feet or swapping improbable stories. Each of them looked toward the door as

Ray Hardin, followed by Wally Chambers, came in.

Sully Parker and Brian Akers were not there. Perhaps they had taken Ray's advice and moved on. Ray stood stiffly facing the men and announced, 'I'd like to have a word with you all.'

'Travis Knight already told us,' a scrawny man named McKeever called out. 'You're the big honcho now.'

'Only as far as the trail drive goes,' Ray replied. '*That* is my business. Wycherly has given me the job and I intend to do the best I can for him.'

'Should be easy,' another man, Joe Carleton, called out. 'Can't do no worse than Duke Wycherly.' There was a short burst of mocking laughter.

Ray continued without returning a smile, 'Most of you have been around for awhile and you know the routine. You should probably rest up your best cutting ponies tomorrow, pick yourself the animal you want for your second mount. Make sure your weapons are clean and loaded. We don't expect any more or any less trouble than we've had the last few years.'

'How large a string of horses?' George Weber, the wrangler, asked.

'Ten spares should do it,' Ray answered, 'after every man has his own two picked out.'

'That makes a string of thirty or so,' Weber said. 'I'll need a helper.'

'Who'd you have last year?'

'Wes Lincoln, but he's drifted on.'

'Pick your own man from those who want the job,' Ray told him.

There were a dozen small questions to be answered,

which Ray tried to respond to with patience and the experience of years on the range. By the time Wally and Ray sat down to the table, everyone seemed satisfied. The steaks they were served were a little dry, half-burnt from being kept waiting, but they tasted fine. Ray and Wally stretched out on their own bunks after eating and pursued sleep.

It had been a good day; the settling night was peaceful, broken only by the occasional snore of a man, decorated by the chirping of crickets and cicadas outside. A peaceful night . . . but Ray's revolver was never far from his hand; there were still predators prowling and morning would bring a new set of problems.

Ray rose from his bunk early the following morning. He did not feel particularly well rested. The solace he had expected after spending so many nights out on open ground had eluded him. He sat up with aching joints and his eyes blurry. Was he already over the hill? He sat on his bunk blinking into the predawn darkness. Most of the hands had already eaten and gone. Knight would have them working early and hard on this last day.

The youngsters had risen with the rooster's crow, eaten their breakfast, and were now saddled and ready to go to work. Ray walked toward the front door of the bunkhouse, holding a hand to the small of his back. Was this how it felt to grow old? What would he do once he was no longer able to fork his bronc and contribute a hard day's work?

He had been having these morning thoughts more

and more frequently lately. With a cup of coffee, Ray stepped out onto the porch to watch the awakening ranch. Smoke rose from both the big house and the guest house. Breakfast was being prepared. A few of the hands were straggling out on horseback, joking or silent according to their natures. Ray recognized Jimmy Polk and Jason Wright even at a distance as they headed toward the herd. At the rear of the big house a couple of men were loading the chuck wagon with food, water, emergency medical supplies, extra blankets and ammunition. Cooky had been at this for nearly twenty years, he knew what was needed. The job of a trail cook was grossly underestimated. Planning a meal for twenty men every day is not a simple task even if they are all under a roof, let alone out on open prairie where everything has to be set up hastily.

On top of that, it was Cooky's job to do what doctoring he could for everything from a man with a bad stomach or split finger to wounds from a steer-goring, broken limbs and bullet wounds. He doubted that Cooky welcomed spring drives eagerly.

Ray had nothing planned for the day, and for that he was grateful. Tomorrow they would be driving five hundred steers into wild country where they had had much trouble before, but worrying about that today would do nothing to solve the problems of a long drive.

Ray Hardin went back into the bunkhouse as the eastern sky colored, poured himself a fresh cup of coffee and began to dress more carefully.

There had been a bowl of hard-boiled eggs on the table, Ray knew from the scattering of shells, but it was empty now. Many of the cowboys took the leftover eggs with them to be eaten on the range.

There was still half of a sheet of baked cornbread and a few dry slices of fried ham on platters, and Ray gratefully devoured some of this food while finishing his coffee.

He stepped out once more onto the porch, which was now bathed in cool yellow sunshine. It was only then that he realized he had not seen Wally yet that morning. He was a fine boss, a fine friend. Not knowing what to do with himself he wandered toward the stables to see to his paint and Bess, the mule, although undoubtedly they were fine and comfy.

Travis Knight passed him, raising a gloved hand in acknowledgment. Knight was apparently resting his favorite cutting horse, and was sitting a deep-chested chestnut with touches of white on the tips of its ears and a white splotch on the end of its muzzle. Ray decided he should give some thought to selecting his own second mount for the drive.

Entering the stable he found Wally Chambers pacing up and down aimlessly past the horse stalls. The man didn't look as if he had slept well.

'What are you up to, Wally?' Ray asked as he approached. Wally's head jerked toward him.

'Oh, hello, Ray. I was just considering.'

'Considering what?'

'Well, the fact is that I wanted to go see Kata and try to explain to her that I was going to be away for a little while.'

'Well, why don't you?'

'It's awfully early,' Wally said.

'I saw smoke rising from the chimney – they're up by now.'

'I guess so, Ray. It's just that I don't know how to explain things.'

'You try, that's all. Wally, don't tell me that you've suddenly gotten shy about talking to the girl.'

'It's not that,' Wally protested, 'it's just that . . . Ray, will you go along with me?'

'Sure, if you like,' Ray said, and Wally smiled, if weakly. Ray thought that he understood a part of it. Things were much different now than they had been in the wild country where Wally had been the girl's protector, her savior. Now Wally had to go away for awhile. Perhaps Kata would discover in his absence that she no longer needed his protection.

That could have been it; Ray was only guessing. Together they stepped out into the bright morning sunlight. A few brown chickens were scratching in front of the house. The big black dog, Bear, lay on the porch with his head on his front paws, but he did not growl or stir. Probably he was too exhausted to do so after yesterday's double run.

Ray and Wally stopped ten feet from the porch. 'Well, go ahead, Wally,' Ray encouraged.

'You're not coming in with me?'

'I don't see what I could contribute. Go on – Kata is probably wondering where you are.' He gave Wally a gentle shove. Ray watched as Wally stepped up onto the porch, removed his hat and knocked. The door swung open and Wally entered the house.

Ray hesitated. He had nowhere else to go, so he decided to wait around until Wally had finished his conversation. That could take some time, Ray considered, smiling. He was remembering the two taking their bath together in the pond along the trail home.

TEN

'You're just standing around looking aimless. No work to do?' a voice from beside the house said, breaking off Ray's thoughts. He turned to find Josie Wycherly there, a straw hat on her head, a burlap sack in one hand, a trowel in the other. She had been out early, digging up weeds from around the house.

'Mornin',' Ray said, touching his hat brim. 'I'm afraid that I'm just following my instructions – doing nothing at all today.'

'Oh, that's right,' Josie said with a bright smile. 'The spring drive starts tomorrow.'

'That's right.'

'I hope you boys don't run into as much trouble as last year.'

'So do I, but there's no predicting.'

'Are you doing nothing today, or just really doing nothing?' Josie asked, looking up at Ray.

'I don't quite understand you.'

Josie laughed. 'This is what I mean: I've been trying to put up a clothes-line in the backyard. I've got the posts and crossbars, wire. I'm just not tall enough to get it done. I could use some help.'

'A clothes-line?' Ray squinted at the girl through the glare of morning sunlight. 'There are already a few behind your house.'

'I thought that the little house should have one of its own. Come on, I'll show you my problem.'

The weeding, a new clothes-line; as he followed Josie around the side of the house, Ray felt like he had to ask, 'Are you planning on moving into the guest house permanently?'

She glanced back across her shoulder as they continued on their way. 'You must know the rule here – the little house is for guests and visiting family unless one of us gets married and chooses to stay on at the Broken W.'

'Then I assume you're not planing on that?' Ray asked, and Josie roared with full-throated laughter.

'Me?' Josie said, dropping her bagful of weeds. 'Who would have me?' She poked at her hair, her expression slightly wistful.

'Probably a lot of men,' Ray said seriously, studying her pretty face and fine figure, 'if you could cut down on your wild rides and get along with fewer dogs.'

'The rides,' Josie said, as she showed Ray the materials she had gathered for her project, 'are just to get me out of the house and forget my family's deeper troubles. As for the dogs, I have them and take them into the house to run free at every opportunity just to make my sisters mad.'

'I see,' Ray answered, not sure if he did. All of Josie's

excesses seemed to be rooted in family problems. Maybe Glen Wycherly knew that. Maybe that was one more thing that Ray had not understood about the red-haired girl.

'Lyle came by to see my father this morning about getting you fired off the job,' Josie told him as they set the upright for the line.

'Did he? How'd that conversation go?'

'Well, you should know that their conversations are mostly a matter of Lyle getting excited and shouting at Father about how the Broken W was being mismanaged and how Lyle could do much better if everyone would just step aside.

'And in the end, Father just told him no, and Lyle stalked out with fire in his eyes.' Josie hesitated just a bit. 'I think my brother means to kill you, Ray. You're frustrating his ambitions.'

That wasn't really news to Ray, but having it put flatly like that was nevertheless troubling. Well, at least it was out in the open now. There was nothing Ray could do about it except to see to his own work as well as he could.

The clothes-line was set. The uprights were well braced and the wire strung tautly. Ray told Josie that he had been waiting for Wally and had better go around the house to meet him. She said she was ready to go in and wash up a little, so she walked with him.

As they rounded the corner to the front of the house, the big black dog lifted his head and gave out a snuffly woof. Josie sat beside the black-headed dog, stroking its head.

'Do you know Charlie Dale over at the Bucket Ranch?' Josie asked out of the blue.

Ray nodded. 'I've met him a time or two.'

'He's always admired Bear here. Wanted him as a yard dog.' Josie smiled brightly. 'I might just let him take him.'

Fine, but that was Josie Wycherly's business and none of his. Why had she bothered to tell him? Just making conversation, Ray convinced himself. He turned as Wally, looking happier than he had for awhile, emerged from the house. Kata stood in the doorway, wearing blue jeans and a flannel shirt. Everyone said a brief hello and a briefer goodbye and Wally and Ray Hardin turned toward the bunkhouse. It was nearly time for dinner.

'How did it go, Wally?' Ray asked although his friend's face told him all he needed to know.

'Fine. It took some time counting on my fingers, miming the sun coming up and going down, but Kata seems to understand that I'll be back in a week or so. She didn't seem worried.'

'Good. That's all straightened out, then.'

'For now, Ray. For now.'

A few paces on Ray told Wally, 'I guess Josie is going to get rid of the big black dog.'

'Good thing; the animal's a brute, but why tell me?'

'I don't know. Why did she tell me?' Ray responded.

'You'd know more about that than I would. Me,' Wally said, 'I don't try to outguess women. It doesn't get you anywhere.'

The rest of the day was spent in sheer indolence.

Outside of one visit to the stable to see to his paint pony, which seemed to be growing weary of its enforced idleness, Ray did nothing but clean his guns, nap and eat.

Morning was a different story entirely. Ray was up before dawn and he was not the first man out of his bunk. Ham and corn muffins were being prepared for the men's breakfasts. Travis Knight had already saddled his chestnut horse and it stood waiting patiently at the rail in front of the bunkhouse. Movement inside the bunkhouse was hectic with men dressing, jabbering, cursing as they stamped on their boots and prepared to ride. There was an electric energy about the place. They had been a long time waiting for this conclusion to the year's work of tending the cattle. A cattle drive, even one fraught with danger, was a liberating event. It not only made a man feel useful, but free of daily routine and the mind-numbing work of constantly patrolling the herd as it was bunched. The gather was completed; the drive could begin.

There was nothing finer than delivering the cattle to their terminus, completing the job which had begun the spring before.

Ray Hardin was not the only man feeling that way. Most of the hands were wearing smiles this morning, eager to get started, to shake off dull routine which is bane to a cowhand.

As the sun broke the eastern horizon, spraying the land with gold and the few high, sheer clouds with color, they were in place, ready to move the herd. The steers, all having risen to their feet, now milled and lowed.

They had been angry at being crowded together, but now they would balk at being driven from home range, started out along the long trail. The first few miles would bring the riders their biggest test. There would be many breakouts from the herd by rogue steers who saw no sense in leaving their habitual graze.

The men and their cutting horses would be well tested, but most of them were beyond capable.

'Head 'em up?' Travis Knight asked Ray.

Ray Hardin nodded. 'That's what we're here for.'

Knight signaled to the cowboys, most of whom had been waiting in a bunch behind the herd. Now they spread out and started their ponies forward, most carrying a coiled lariat in their hands to hie the beeves along. They shouted loudly as they progressed, startling the cattle into alertness. That had been their intention.

Already there were a few breakouts, but the riders on their swift, sure-footed ponies urged the steers back into the bunch and eventually one steer assumed the mantle of leader and led the way out onto the southern trail; the rest, some mildly, some reluctantly, followed.

On a grassy knoll to the north Ray saw Glen Wycherly sitting his old white horse, watching. He was not concerned, not there to instruct or criticize, but to observe the object of all of his work driven safely off and into his bank account – as it were. It pleasured the old man to watch the frantic, seemingly chaotic work of his cowhands. They were a skilled, tough bunch who knew their jobs.

Ray lifted a hand to Glen in farewell and started his paint forward toward the men riding drag, figuring they might need some help at the early stages of the drive. There was a huge cloud of white dust which would not settle until hours had passed. This was the reason Cooky and his temporary assistant, Bo Julian, had started their chuck wagon out on the trail at the hour before dawn.

For the men riding drag there was no escape from the billowing dust. Bandannas were tugged up to cover noses and mouths, but that provided little real relief. Eyes were gritty and sore from trying to peer into the dust cloud to keep balky, lagging steers from deserting the herd. Ray rode the morning shift there along with Lenny Polk and Joe Carleton. At noon he would relieve them with another crew.

Travis Knight appeared through the sifting dust as Ray finished nudging a young steer back into the herd. Ray nodded to him and pulled aside a little from the worst of the dust cloud.

'How far?' Knight asked, meaning how far did Ray mean to drive the herd which was yet to be trail-broken on this day.

'I'm not out to set any records,' Ray said through his blue bandanna's mask. There were some trail bosses who tried to impress their owners with how quickly they could finish their drives, irritating men and cattle alike. 'I think the pond at Old Post Springs is far enough for today. We should be there by mid-afternoon. Their legs will be weary enough, and they'll have water and grass, so there shouldn't be much scattering.'

Knight nodded his agreement. 'I'll send Jason Wright out ahead to tell Cooky to hold up there and start fixing our supper.'

'Right,' Ray Hardin said, above the rumble of thousands of hoofs. 'While he's doing that, tell Wright to keep an eye on the land around us.'

'You expecting trouble this early on?' Travis Knight asked.

'No. I'm not expecting anything except that there will be trouble of some kind before we reach Fort Davis.'

And if someone – like Blue Moon Priest – coveted the herd, they might figure to surprise the Broken W riders early on the drive when they would not be expecting it. Rustlers usually preferred to let the cattlemen do the difficult work of trail-breaking the steers before they struck, but you never could tell.

Not reluctantly Ray gave up his spot riding drag to McKeever, sent back by Knight or perhaps by Wally Chambers, who was riding point. Ray drifted out onto the right flank of the herd, moving away from it a little so as to have a clearer view of the entire operation. As he sat a low rise cluttered with sage and yucca, he looked around wondering when the herd would be hit and who would be responsible for it.

They had never driven a herd along the entire southern trail without being raided. The temptation was too great. Usually they had gotten past the raiders with only minimal losses in their cattle count. The temptation was great, but the thought of facing an all-out battle with twenty tough, loyal cowhands was a deterrent to most poachers. The standing order in case of such an attack had been issued by Glen Wycherly himself and repeated by Ray at the start of the drive: 'If they hit you hard, forget about the cattle; they can be gathered again. Grab your guns and take it to them.'

Would Jack Priest be willing to take such a risk with his gang of bank robbers, street fighters, highwaymen and raiders over cattle he would have to drive long and far, rebrand and sell? Ray didn't know. He had met with Blue Moon but had no idea what the man would attempt. He knew that cattle were not Jack Priest's choice of targets. They were trouble. If a bank were cracked or a stagecoach held up, the job was over as soon as the money had been collected. Cattle were a much more dicey proposition. They would have to be driven, tended, brands changed, a purchaser found. Outlaws did not care for ranch work as a rule, otherwise they would not be doing what they were for a living.

Lyle Wycherly. Now he was a different story. He seemed to be intent not only on profit, but on ruining his father. If Blue Moon were not backing him with two dozen men would he have the nerve to try it on his own? And why would Jack Priest back Lyle? Could it be that the outlaw chief had his eyes on the Broken W himself, was using Lyle only to eventually take the ranch over as a different and far better base for his operations?

Ray shook his head, wishing that his mind was better at solving puzzles. For the time being all that he could do was get the herd through to Fort Davis. He wondered if, despite having given his word, despite the threats of Blue Moon he wouldn't be better off telling the army about the outlaw camp.

Either option seemed to somehow, if vaguely, put the ranch, Glen Wycherly and the women at more risk.

It stank. The cattle stank. Ray wasn't too sure that his entire life and future didn't stink. He decided that he was spending too much time alone, brooding. He started the paint horse down the slope, his concentration only on getting the herd to Old Post Springs. It was a difficult day for the men. There were more than a few balky steers determined to get back to their usual grass and water, but Ray did not think they lost more than a couple of these.

Night camp was made early. The cattle bunched up against the pond with new grass around accepted their lot. As the evening began to settle, there was still a problem of bedding them down in these unusual circumstances. Ray had Travis Knight assign three extra men to ride night herd. The first night was when the steers were most likely to strike out on their own.

Cooky had their meal prepared before the herd had even arrived, and settling down to eat beneath a scraggly willow tree as the western sky purpled, a tired Ray Hardin began to have hopes that things would go well for them. Wally Chambers joined him after awhile, carrying two tin cups of coffee. The two men had not seen much of each other over the course of the day. Wally had been at the point, guiding the drive.

'Everything all right?' Ray asked Wally.

'Well enough. Two of the boys got into it after one of them accused the other over forcing his pony up against the herd. I told them we didn't have the time for it – unless they wanted to dismount and wait until the herd passed by.'

'They didn't.'

'They didn't. Say, Ray, do you want me to follow the old route all the way to Fort Davis?'

'Why not?' Ray asked.

'No reason,' Wally answered, 'except that I thought you might want to veer a little toward the east. Now that we know where the outlaw trail is, where they would have to come from if they wanted the herd, it might give us more warning if we saw them coming.'

'We can't avoid them if they want to come after us, Wally. Stick to the old trail.'

'All right.' Wally rose, smiling. 'Whatever you say, boss. How far do you want to go tomorrow? These steers aren't exactly trail-broken yet.'

'Can we make the big pond? You know,' Ray couldn't resist adding, 'the swimming hole? What's that: fifteen, twenty miles on?'

'If that's what you want to try.' Wally shrugged. 'We'll have some weary men and some trail-beat steers when we get there, though.'

'The men are getting paid for the job, and I'm not asking the cows what they want,' Ray said.

'Getting hard, are you?' Wally grinned.

'Just trying to do the job Glen Wycherly set for me the best way I can. I'll talk to Knight later and tell him what I have in mind for tomorrow.'

By the time Ray turned into his bed, the camp-fires were burning low but still glowing brightly. The evening had cooled, but it was a pleasant coolness after the heat of the day. A couple of the boys sat around singing old camp songs. They weren't very good when it came to harmony, but no one minded. After awhile the fires burned to embers and the singers went to their own beds. There were handfuls of silver stars sprinkled across the dark, clear sky. Ray spotted a small pack of coyotes lurking, but these would cause no trouble. They had more sense than to enter the large camp. Morning would bring them back scavenging for any discarded food.

Ray's mouth opened in a jaw-breaking yawn, and he gave up any effort to stay awake longer as he rolled up more tightly in his blanket.

The moon had risen and passed over, leaving its ghostly white memory floating above the western horizon, when Ray rose in the hour before dawn, rolled his blankets and began outfitting his paint pony. Cooky, up first as usual, had been active. Ray could smell coffee coming to a boil.

No one was eager to chat on this cool morning. They nodded to each other and went silently about their business of saddling whatever horse they meant to use on this day. An hour on they had the herd up and ready to travel. The steers, some seeming to be sleep-dazed, were moved out with relative ease and began their bovine plodding eastward.

The morning sun was brilliant, and Ray rode with his hat tugged low, trying to watch all the activity and the far country at once.

The land was long, white, almost featureless. The Holden Range to the north still bulked large, casting long, heavy shadows. They lost their first steers around noon. Ray had returned to ride drag for awhile, relieving McKeever. Young Lenny Polk was his companion. Polk suddenly lifted a pointing finger and, looking that way, Ray saw three men holding rifles, a wagon drawn up behind them.

'What are they after?' Polk wondered.

'What we seem to have plenty of and they none,' Ray replied.

They were poor desert homesteaders, living rough in a hard land. Every year since Ray had hired on there had been a few of these wretched men along the trail, hoping for a lame steer to fall out or one to wander from the herd. Glen Wycherly's instructions were clear when it came to this type: 'Let them have a few. It's good for ranch relations and they may have family, children at home who haven't eaten meat for months.'

'Want me to drive them off?' Lenny Polk, who was new on the Broken W, asked, almost eagerly.

'No. Cut out a three of the stragglers and leave them behind.'

'Are you serious?' Polk asked.

'Serious,' Ray told him.

'You're the boss. Anyway, a few of these lagging cows have practically made me carry them along the trail. I'm tired of pushing them back where they belong.'

Ray watched as Polk shouldered one of the dawdlers with his horse's shoulder and pushed it toward open country. Two others were sent to follow with a rap from Polk's coiled lariat. The ragged homesteaders did not rush forward, nor did they so much as lift a hand in gratitude. Ray had expected no such demonstration.

The herd dragged on.

The next day was very little different. Endless white vista, clouds of accompanying dust, dry, glaring heat. Ray was a little surprised that they had not come across a single Indian as yet. Maybe the army was doing a better job of distributing their beef allotments these days.

The Broken W herd was not yet trail-broken, perhaps, but the animals were weary now. They simply walked forward with few complaints, trudging toward their fate. To rest his paint Ray occasionally rode a strapping young palomino from the Broken W string. The three-year-old was eager, high-stepping and more than a little cantankerous. Nevertheless it could cover some ground and that was all that was required. It was necessary for Ray to ride to the point of the herd to talk with Wally, to drop back along the flanks to see how each man was doing and then position himself once again at drag to discuss matters with Polk or whoever had rotated there. No man was condemned to ride drag and eat dust for eight to ten hours a day.

That night they made their camp along what was called Dutchman Creek. Water flowed freely from the uplands here and the creek ran wide and cool. The cattle were lined up along the stream to drink when Wally caught up with Ray again.

'You know where we are?' Wally asked, swinging down from his weary dun pony.

'Approximately. Don't you?' Ray asked, a little surprised by the question.

'I thought I'd remind you,' Wally said. 'That notch

we passed an hour or so ago is the end of the east trail out of the Poconos.'

'Yes,' Ray said, 'it is.'

'We can't be more than five, ten miles from Blue Moon's stronghold.'

'I know it,' Ray replied. 'Wally, I can't help but think that Jack Priest has gotten out of the cattle business.'

'Because we've already ridden past the trail and he let us go on?'

'That and other reasons.' Namely, that Blue Moon hadn't seemed all that eager to continue his working relationship with Lyle Wycherly.

'I hope you're right, Ray,' Wally said, with some concern showing on his face. 'For myself I'd be pleased to finish this entire drive without having to fire my gun.'

'We might just make it.' Ray glanced toward the darkening sky. 'Besides, any rustlers planning to work at night are crazy. The cattle will scatter and you can't find them in the darkness. If you wait and try to round them all up the following day it's as difficult as if you have had to do the job by yourself in the first place and with cowboys sniping at you.

'No, Wally, I don't think we have anything to worry about tonight.'

Like most predictions, this one was far off the mark.

ELEVEN

In the hour after midnight the raiders came with a fury and a mad rush as if the Devil were at their heels. Their intention had obviously been to hit fast and hard while most of the crew were sleeping. They had struck from the rear, away from the gathered herd and the night riders working there. They had come, that is, from the direction of the eastern trail to the outlaw camp of Blue Moon Priest.

The problem for the raiders was that they were as night-blind as the sleeping cowboys who rose from their beds, guns in hand to repel the sneak attack. Only shadows and the red gun-flashes could be seen in the night. Ray heard a man cry out in pain, but could not see who it was nor tell which side he was on as the outlaws' horses stampeded wildly through the camp. The horses reflexively leaped over the sleeping or rising men, but the men were targets for the raiders' guns. Ray saw one man shot at point-blank range. Again he could not see who the man was, but he was definitely a Broken W man and he was definitely dead after taking a shot full in the chest.

The outlaws reached the far side of the camp, apparently without suffering any losses. They immediately turned their ponies and raced through the camp again. This time, however, the Broken W cowboys were armed, braced and ready to fire back. They were not all wide awake, but most of them could use their guns well even in their sleep.

The herd of dark horses raced toward them. Ray, who had not had time to find decent cover, fired from his knees, tagged one of the silhouetted raiders as he rode past, heard him groan, saw him fall. A second rider was coming directly at him, having seen the brilliant red and golden muzzle-flash of Ray's Colt. He seemed to have it in mind to ride Ray Hardin down.

Ray shot once, hit nothing and then went to his back against the cold, hard ground. As the outlaw's horse leaped over him out of instinct, Ray fired his pistol up into the horse's belly. It was none of the horse's fault, but Ray had no choice. The horse buckled up immediately and rolled, head first to the ground, whickering wildly, legs thrust out, kicking at the sky. The rider did not rise. His neck had been broken in the fall.

Across the camp revolvers and rifles roared. Horses milled in excited confusion. The men on the ground, braced and ready, had the better of it as the raiders tried to fire back from their saddles atop the confused, panicked animals. Ray saw a raider fall from the saddle and another slump forward to spur his horse away as he clung to its neck in a desperate wish to escape. He fell from the pony a hundred feet on and did not move again.

As the camp cleared, Ray rose to his feet, automatically reloading his Colt with the cartridges from his gunbelt. There were men down, wounded, but he could not tell who they were or how many had been shot.

The only surprise, he was thinking, was that the herd itself had not been hit by those reckless men. Then from across Dutchman Creek he heard a volley of muffled shots, saw one gun flare in the darkness. He hurried to find his paint pony, forgetting he had left it with the string. The young palomino was there, however. The colt was jittery, wild-eyed, but Ray managed to saddle it hastily and swing aboard, feeling that he was moving in slow motion – much too late to be of any help to the men riding night herd.

He was almost correct. Splashing across the creek, he arrived at the herd as most of the intense fighting had stilled. Then a man appeared out of the night, rushing at Ray. The raider's hat had been lost and his horse was lathered. He was looking back across his shoulder as he spurred his horse furiously. That did not mean that he was unready to fight; the two men faced each other on horseback and the bandit's pistol came up. Ray Hardin was already set and he triggered off his Winchester rifle, lifting the raider from the saddle. The horse, a neat-looking little blue roan, shrugged the rider from his back and ambled away, reins trailing. Ray's own palomino, unused to these violent man-games, shuddered beneath him.

'Ray!' Travis Knight called, as the Broken W foreman

stumbled toward Ray Hardin. Knight's left arm was dangling uselessly at his side. Obviously it had been broken. There was pain on his drawn face.

'How bad was it out here?' Ray wanted to know.

'Pretty bad. Two men down. McKeever and Jason Wright. The cattle are pretty much scattered.'

'There's nothing to be done about that now,' Ray said, looking toward the dark skies. 'We'll have to collect those we can in the morning and figure on a short sale.'

'Who's that?' asked Travis Knight, wincing in pain. He was holding his broken arm and squinting into the darkness where the dead man still lay.

'I've no idea except that he didn't seem to like me.'

Knight went that way with Ray Hardin walking his horse along. Knight squatted over the body, rolled it to one side and grunted. 'It's Brian Akers,' he said. 'Damned traitor! I guess it's bad form to kick a dead man, isn't it, Ray?'

'If it makes you feel any better, do it. I won't mind.'

'He's just not worth it,' Travis Knight muttered. Moving carefully they managed to get Knight up behind Ray on the palomino. They splashed back across the creek and went directly to Cooky's wagon where he and Bo Julian, his young assistant, were tending to the wounded by lantern light.

'Another one?' Cooky growled.

'It's Travis Knight, Cooky. He's got a broken arm. Help me get him down, will you.'

Cooky, whose white cook's apron was already stained with blood, gestured to Julian and the two managed to slide Knight from the palomino's back. There were other wounded men standing around in obvious discomfort, and there were two lying in the wagon, dead or badly wounded Ray could not tell.

A full assessment would have to wait until morning. Ray swung down from his horse and walked across the camp to where his bed had been made. He had no intention of trying to fall asleep again. Ray placed a blanket across his shoulders and sat staring at the haggard night.

When the cattle were gathered in the morning, Wally estimated that although they had done their best at least fifty steers were missing from the herd. The crew and cattle were now truly trail-weary and Ray called a halt to the drive for the day.

After the lost day, they pushed the herd through to Fort Davis the following afternoon, reaching it as sundown colored the western skies with hazy purple and a flush of crimson. Ray had been riding at the point in anticipation of their arrival. A young, fresh-faced lieutenant named Sabat rode out to meet them and, after asking directions from Lenny Polk, drifted over to meet with Ray astride his paint pony.

'I've got men at the cattle pens ready to help you as best they can,' Lieutenant Sabat told him. Looking at Ray's weary, discouraged face, he asked, 'How did it go this year?'

Ray answered, 'Worse than some, better than others. Have you got a surgeon on the post still?'

'Yes, we do,' Sabat said. 'Bring him some work, did you?'

'I'm afraid so. Also the herd is going to be a little short.'

'We're glad to have them anyway,' Sabat said. 'Give Mr Wycherly our thanks.'

Ray nodded. 'I will. Do you men want to count the cattle now – it's almost dark?'

'Now,' the lieutenant said. 'It's easier when they go through the gates than after they're in the pens and begin milling,' Sabat told him. 'As soon as we've got them put to bed I'll deliver the tally to the disbursement officer and he'll make out a bank draft in Mr Wycherly's name.

'For the rest of you – I know you don't wish to do any more traveling tonight. I'll find you a bed in the visiting officers' quarters and see that your men have bunks in one of the barracks. They'll be free to have a few beers from the sutler's stores. Compliments of the US Army.'

Quite a few of the men accepted the army's compliments freely as Ray found out the following morning when he tried to rouse them for the return to the Broken W. They were grouchy and slow to respond to his summons. They had had a long trail drive, all the beer they could drink and a peaceful night in army cots behind the walls of Fort Davis.

Wally Chambers shouted at two of the more reluctant men, 'If you like it here so much, join the army – if they'll have you!'

Around ten o'clock in the morning they rode out of Fort Davis in a loose bunch. Travis Knight, Joe Carleton and a few of the others had been left behind so that their wounds would have time to heal. The men had no fear of being attacked again – they had nothing left that any raiders might want.

Ray Hardin was not so sure. Along the trail he told Wally Chambers, 'I've got that bank draft in my pocket.'

'I know. So what? No outlaw can walk into the bank and cash it. It's in Glen Wycherly's name.'

'Or someone with his power of attorney.'

'Who are you talking about?' Wally asked. He was perplexed.

'Patricia Wycherly,' Ray said. 'She virtually controls the ranch's finances. Glen has given her that authority.'

'And you expect that meek woman to ride down on us with her guns blazing?' Wally scoffed.

'She has associates,' Ray said soberly, stilling his friend's amusement.

'What are you saying? Who do you mean? Not Duke Wycherly!'

'Why not? Lyle wants everything, and he wants it now. He's the one who raided us, not Blue Moon Priest.'

'How did you come to that conclusion?' Wally asked.

'For one thing Brian Akers was riding with them. I don't think he suddenly abandoned Lyle to join up with Blue Moon. For another, those men weren't after the herd. They were there to raise havoc, kill as many Broken W riders as they could, maybe force a few of the others to quit the ranch. And, there's something Josie told me. She thinks that both of her sisters are involved in stripping the Broken W of its assets, driving it into ruin and sharing what's left.'

'You believed her?'

'I believe her,' Ray said firmly.

'Snagging that check would go a long way toward ruining the ranch,' Wally said thoughtfully. 'If Duke were to get his hands on it and pass it on to Patricia, they'd have a substantial profit for themselves.' He shook his head. 'But, Ray, we can't be sure of any of this.'

'There's little a man can be sure of, Wally. All I'm saying is I doubt that Lyle Wycherly is through yet.'

'You'd better tuck that check away somewhere safer,' Wally suggested.

'So that Lyle won't be able to find it after he kills me?' Ray asked with a dry smile.

'All right!' Wally said. 'So we ride with our eyes open and our guns at the ready.'

'A better idea,' Ray agreed.

However, the long, white days passed by without incident. Finally reaching the Broken W again after twelve days on the trail, the men lifted their saddles from their weary ponies and made their stiff-legged way toward the bunkhouse to rest. Ray Hardin was as trail-weary as any of them; however, his work was not quite done. The sky was beginning to color in the west. A cool, slight breeze was blowing, ruffling the leaves of the big oak trees in front of the house. Ray handed off the reins to his paint to the wrangler, Joe Weber, and made his way toward the house afoot, passing the smaller house. He wondered how the women were getting along, but that consideration would have to wait until after his meeting with Glen Wycherly.

Fifty yards on, passing through the oak grove, he came up against them. Lyle Wycherly and Sully Parker were standing before him, blocking the path. Somehow it did not surprise Ray to see Louise Wycherly standing to one side, her arms crossed under a black shawl she was wearing over a black dress. Her eyes were cold, but sharp as steel.

'I'll take it now, Hardin,' Lyle Wycherly said, holding out a hand. Sully Parker, rifle in his hands, was watching Ray eagerly. He wanted Ray dead, wanted to be the one to do it. Sully stood awkwardly; his thigh, which Kata had wounded, was still troubling him, always would.

'You'll take it all right,' Ray answered, 'if you don't get out of my way.'

'You can't win, Hardin. Sully's practically got you in his sights, and I'm quicker on the draw than you could ever hope to be.'

'And Louise has a stiletto, I assume.' The joke went nowhere. None of the other three was in the mood for humor. Louise did tighten her grip on her shawl as if it could protect her somehow.

'Where's Patricia? In fixing the books?'

'I'm through talking with you, Hardin; hand over the bank draft, or die where you stand.'

Ray caught a flicker of movement out of the corner of his eye. His expression did not change as he said, 'I won't betray the old man's trust. As for dying— Hell, a man only lives once anyway.'

Louise Wycherly went ghost-white. Maybe she had assumed that Ray would not be willing to die over a piece of paper, not with two armed men facing him.

She couldn't know that Ray Hardin had been in worse situations.

Lyle Wycherly tried a snap draw. His thumb seemed to miss the hammer of the Colt he wore. Ray's draw was slower, cleaner. Lyle buckled up, fired his pistol into the ground and threw his head back in anguish, belly-shot. Sully Parker shouldered his rifle but never fired it. Simultaneously with Ray Hardin's shot, the pistol in Wally Chambers's hand barked savagely and Sully threw his hands into the air, his rifle flying free. The big man howled a full-throated roar, turned and hobbled off into the oaks. His run resembled a crippled duck waddling.

'I got him in his good leg,' Wally said, coming forward. 'Not much of a shot, but . . . I never seen a man trying to limp on both legs at once.'

'He's done,' Ray said. 'He'll never ride a horse or walk right again.' He nodded toward Lyle Wycherly, who had stopped his writhing, panicked objection to death. 'Take care of getting rid of the remains, will you?'

Then Ray walked past Louise Wycherly, who stood trembling from head to foot, her face ashen, her eyes holding utter disbelief.

Ray said, 'Young ladies shouldn't play rough games.' Then he walked on, heading for the big house to deliver the army's bank draft to Glen Wycherly. He would have to talk to the old man, explain everything that he knew of what had happened. How he would go about that he wasn't sure, but somehow he thought that Glen Wycherly would understand matters even if he did not care for the way it had turned out. There was no movement or sound left in the twilight-shadowed oak grove but the high-pitched, mournful wailing of Louise Wycherly, who had just witnessed the death of her dreams.

'Aren't you going to put on a clean shirt?' Wally Chambers asked. He was standing with one boot propped up on the steps of the bunkhouse, trying to polish his worn boots with a rag.

'This is the cleanest one I have,' Ray Hardin said. 'Want to wait for me to do some laundry?'

'No,' Wally said, tossing the rag aside. 'Let's get on over there. The two women invited us to dinner; let's deliver our appetites.'

Wally started off toward the little house where smoke rose in lazy curlicues from the iron stovepipe into the sundown skies. Ray, on second thought, picked up the rag Wally had tossed and gave his own boots the once-over.

When Wally tapped on the door it opened almost immediately. A dark woman in a pale-green gown, her hair pinned up on her head, smiled at him. Beyond her Wally saw a red-headed girl wearing a silky, peach-colored dress, a strand of pearls around her graceful neck.

The woman who had opened the door continued to smile.

'Welcome home, Wally,' Kata said. Wally backed away, stuttering something. Ray had arrived at the foot of the porch steps. Wally stepped down to grip his arm at the elbow.

'Ray,' Wally said in a shaky voice, 'we've been through a lot in our time, haven't we?'

'Quite a bit,' Ray Hardin agreed. 'But we've always managed to fight our way out of trouble.'

'True,' Wally agreed, 'but, Ray, I think we're about to walk into something where we have no chance. None at all.'